Sunflower Bride

By Linda Sealy Knowles

Copyright 2019 Linda Sealy Knowles
Forget Me Not Romances, a division of Winged Publications

All rights reserved. No part of this publication may be reproduced, stored in a retrieval system, or transmitted in any form or by any means, with the exception of brief quotations in printed reviews.

This book is a work of fiction. The characters in this story are the product of the author's imagination and are completely fictitious.

All rights reserved.

ISBN-13: 978-1-947523-48-7
ISBN-10: 1-947523-48-1

Dedication

Reba Overstreet Smith
One of my closest friends, with whom I shared twelve years of wonderful day-to-day thoughts and dreams. Someone I miss seeing every day, but I know she's still very near.

Chapter One

1870

"Come over here, Elly, and read this," Ruby Jackson said and tapped her stubby finger on the telegraph office bulletin board in Leesville, Louisiana.

"For goodness sakes, Ruby, let me read it." Eleanor Eddy pushed Ruby's hand out of the way. She sidestepped her friend's full-figure body.

"It says we can sign up to leave this godforsaken town on the wagon train," Ruby said as three men staggered past them, throwing kisses in their general direction. "We can have a new life, a new beginning." She glared at the men, then smiled at Elly.

Elly stared down at Ruby's rosy cheeks. "I don't need a new beginning. We work in different jobs. I'm not judging you for the way you have to earn your money, but I teach school and manage my cleaning business." Maybe not a real teacher with a certificate, but educated after all. She'd filled in because the school board couldn't get anyone else to answer their advertisements.

"Two jobs you hate, if what you have told me these past few months is true." Ruby tilted her moon face up toward Elly's.

"I like teaching, but I don't have any control over my students.

I can't make the unruly ones behave and have to get permission from one of the school-board members before I can discipline any of them. For some reason, I feel like I'm being watched by the townspeople. It's like the ladies are just waiting for me to smile at a strange man or go for a walk with someone, or even be seen out with you. I'm sorry, Ruby, but someone will have something to say about us being seen together." She shrugged. "I don't care. You're my best friend."

"Well, why don't we sign up and get out of this rough town?"

"Ruby, for goodness sakes. Read it again." Elly couldn't believe that Ruby had missed the most important part of the notice. "It's asking women to sign a contract to become mail-order brides. Men are waiting for brides in Sunflower, Texas. I personally don't want to be married. You need to think about this plan before you sign a contract that would place you in a more unpleasant situation than you have here."

"Well, I need to get out of this town—out from under Wild Bill's authority. He's placing more demands on us girls and paying us less. But I'm too afraid to venture into unknown territory by myself," Ruby said, peering up at her with doe-like eyes as they headed to Big Jim's Café for a cup of tea.

Eleanor Eddy smoothed raven strands of hair out of her eyes. Then she pushed open her parasol and strolled arm in arm with her young friend, noting the frowns of the townspeople who knew her. By nightfall, the school superintendent would be calling on her, demanding that she be careful whom she spent time with, especially in public. She could hear him now. "No decent woman keeps company with one of Wild Bill's young whores."

Elly knew that her days as a substitute schoolteacher were nearly over. She'd heard the gossip that the superintendent had received a letter from a male teacher seeking a position here in Leesville.

Elly and Ruby entered the sweet-smelling bakery and café and took a table next to the sunny window. "How can I help you ladies today," Big Jim, the owner, said with a grin on his face until he noticed Ruby. A dark frown crossed his face.

"Now, Miss," he said and cleared his throat. Two well-dressed ladies gave him and Elly a sharp look as they marched past the table with their chins held high, mumbling under their breath loud enough for both of them to hear, "He allows all kinds of trash in this establishment."

Big Jim began again. "Now, Miss, Ruby, is it?" Before she could respond, he continued, "You know that I cannot serve you; that is, if I want to keep a proper business. You must leave now."

"I'm sorry, Big Jim," Ruby said, lowering her eyes. Her cheeks flamed from embarrassment. "I thought that since I was with Miss Eleanor, you wouldn't mind me coming in for a spot of tea, but I'll be going."

"Ruby, I'm leaving with you. We'll go somewhere else." Like a reigning queen, Elly straightened her vest and smoothed her skirt, took Ruby's elbow, and led her out the door. As they stepped out onto the boardwalk, a massive force bumped into Elly.

The man, taller than the open door, nearly knocked her down. Ruby caught her arm and helped Eleanor regain her balance. "Watch where you're going you, big brute. You nearly pushed me into the muddy street," Eleanor said in her most priggish voice. She snapped her parasol and aimed it toward the stranger's head, shaking it to add emphasis to her words.

"I'm sorry, lady. Name's Tate Maynard." he said, as he dodged her parasol, "but I beg to differ with you. It was you who wasn't watching where you were going."

"Well, I never!" Eleanor straightened her bonnet, then grabbed Ruby's arm. They strode away from the rude man and the close-minded café.

Tate Maynard, ramrod and scout for his father's wagon train, stood grinning at the two ladies who marched like cute little soldiers down the boardwalk until they were out of sight. He laughed to himself and entered the café that smelled of fresh coffee and home-cooked food. He was looking forward to a decent meal, prepared by someone other than his chuck-wagon cook.

Ruby waved good-bye to Elly, who stood in the doorway of Mrs. Duffy's Rooming House, apologizing for causing her too much trouble for one day. They separated and agreed to meet again soon.

As Elly climbed the flight of stairs to her room, she wondered if she would ever stop missing the small frame house at the edge of town where she had lived as long as she could remember. Life had been good—once.

The door was ajar. She paused and eased it open. Immediately her eyes went to her bed. A figure with long legs was sprawled across it. Timmy, her younger brother. *Just what I need,* thought Elly as she approached the bed.

She stopped and surveyed the room. In the middle of the floor was a carpetbag that she guessed was Timmy's. His big boots lay where he'd taken them off. He'd probably told Mrs. Duffy some wild tale to convince her to let him into her room. Yes, Timmy was a smooth talker, and a gambler and a drinker. She had stopped supporting him once he refused to help her with the delivery of the wash to her customers. "I'm a grown man now," he snorted one afternoon. "I ain't no old washwoman."

That evening, Elly decided that since he declared himself a grown man, he could care for himself. She ordered him out of their house and demanded he get himself a real job because her days of supporting him were over. She always regretted kicking him out of their home, but a twenty-year-old man needed to support himself.

"Timmy, wake up," Elly shook his shoulder. He grabbed the

pillow, pulled it under his chin, and opened and closed his mouth. "Lord, please help me. I can't believe he's going to be a man just like our pa," she mumbled. "Timmy, get up," Elly called more forcibly.

This time her brother shook her hand away and grumbled for her to leave him alone.

Elly grabbed the pillow and hit him in the stomach with it. "Get up," she practically screamed at him.

"What?" Timmy finally opened his eyes and glared at his sister, who stood holding the pillow that had struck him in the midsection.

"Get up and tell me what you're doing here, piled up like a royal prince on my bed—a bed that I work hard all month long to sleep in." Why wasn't he over at Wild Bill's Saloon in his rented room?

"Sis, don't start that business again about me being a lazy bum. I work long, hard hours." He sat up on the side of her bed, rubbing his eyes. His face looked like it had a thirty-six-hour growth of beard.

"If you call sitting at a gambling table for twelve hours a day a job, then I hope you can show some money for all that time," Elly said. She circled around and kicked a boot out of the center of the room.

"Stop yelling."

"Tell me how much money you won the last time you sat at the tables?" She had already guessed he was broke because he had come crawling back to her. When he didn't give a response, she asked another one. "What do you want this time, Timmy. I have no money to hand over to you. I'm going to need all the money I've saved to tide me over while I seek another job to support myself."

"Are you thinking about leaving this town to get another job?" He stretched his arms.

"I may not leave here, but I am thinking about a different kind of job for myself. I don't have a teacher's certificate, but everything I do in this town is scrutinized. I can't take a Sunday afternoon stroll with a friend or be seen speaking with a gentleman in public. Every move I make is dissected for fear that I might do something that would embarrass the townspeople."

"You can't just quit your job. What are you going to do for money?" After adjusting his pants and shirt, he grabbed his boot and slipped it on over his sockless foot. Hopping across the room, he shoved his foot into the other boot, then stuffed a few things in his front pocket.

"Sure, you want me to have a job so you can come 'borrowing' from me whenever you need something." She picked up her hairbrush and rearranged it on her dresser.

"I just need a place to stay for a few nights and a good hot bath. After a game or two, I'll get my own place—again. Old Mrs. Duffy downstairs said I could wait until you got home, but I have to leave before dinner."

"She doesn't allow dinner or overnight guests in anyone's room, and especially men taking baths in her house. You cannot stay here with me. What happened to your room over at Wild Bill's?"

Timmy didn't reply to his sister's question about his lodging arrangements at the saloon. He probably thought it was none of her business. "Come on, Sis, and let me sleep on your floor. Mrs. Duffy won't even know I'm here."

"And when she does find out, you and I both will be booted out onto the street. No way are you staying up here with me. Mrs. Duffy has been angry at you for a while. You promised to repair her porch and you never did. Just leave your bag until you get settled somewhere and then come back for it."

Timmy stooped down to see himself in the dresser's mirror and ran his large hands through his dark hair. At twenty-years-old, her handsome brother charmed all the ladies with his quick smile.

"All right. I'm going," he said, glancing at himself one more time in the mirror, "but I'll need a few things out of my bag soon."

He threw her a cocky smile and walked out the door with a little salute.

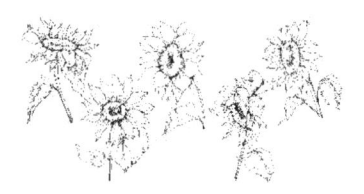

Chapter 2

Elly yawned and stretched after sitting in her straight-back chair for hours preparing lesson plans for the next few days. Time for bed. Her back ached as she donned her nightgown. She was pleased that her brother had not come back, pestering her for lodging and money. Mrs. Duffy and Elly had a good relationship, and she didn't want to take advantage of the kind woman.

Before Elly retired, she lifted her window to allow in what breeze there was on this hot, humid evening. She stared down at the swinging doors of Wild Bill's Saloon. Her pa had worked there for years. He began drinking the liquor that he served and fooling around with the soiled doves who worked in the saloon. Martha, Elly's mama, baked pies for the local bakery and took in wash and ironing for many customers. She was too exhausted to be the loveable wife Pa wanted every morning after work. When he had a bad night, which seemed to be often, he'd take his frustrations out on his wife. As a small child, Elly had heard the beatings and cries from her poor mama. She promised herself that no man would ever mistreat her—she would never marry and let a man have control of her life.

During the night she threw off the bedcovers, struggling to get comfortable. Hours later she drifted into a deep sound sleep.

"Wake up, Miss," shouted a man who shook her arm. Was she dreaming? She opened her eyes. That awful man who nearly pushed her down on the boardwalk was standing over her. She bolted up in her dream, her leg bare from her ankle to the top of her buttocks. Her cotton bloomers had ridden down past her knees. The man must have noticed. He grabbed the top sheet and covered her rump.

"Come on now. Wake up and let's get out." The voice was higher pitched, followed by a loud growl.

"Go away, Timmy. Leave me in peace," she mumbled at her brother who must have returned and wanted money.

"Get up, Miss. We've got to get out of here. The walls are on fire."

Fire, did he said fire? Is something on fire? She couldn't process what he was saying. Shaking her head, she saw the man in her dreams. Or was this a nightmare?

Elly sat up. The man was yelling at her to come with him. The room was as hot as hades and was filling with smoke. Leaping from the bed, she pulled up her underpants and took hold of her robe as the man grabbed her arm. She wiped hot tears from her burning eyes.

"Go, get to the stairs now," he said and shoved her toward the door.

"Wait. I have to get my clothes and my money." She sidestepped the big guy, slid her arms into her thin robe and bent down beside her bed. Feeling under the mattress, she pulled out the tin box and opened it. Empty. "Damnit, that Timmy stole my money," she coughed and slapped the bed.

"Get your fanny in gear, woman. This place is about to cave in around us." Sounds of the crackling fire, falling boards, and windows breaking came from above. Screams came from below.

"I need my clothes," Elly screamed again.

The tall man reached for a carpetbag that was opened sitting by the closet door. Elly was still in a daze, as she whirled around, searching for items to take. She grabbed her hairbrush and her Bible, but the smoke was making it hard to decide what else she should take.

"You're coming with me, woman." He attempted to drag her out of the room, but she slapped his hands. She sidestepped around the big man and jerked her quilt off her bed. She may not have any money, but she wasn't going to leave the only nice thing she had left of her mama's.

Out of patience, he grabbed the old quilt, wrapped it around Elly's body and threw her over his shoulder. He rushed down the staircase as fiery boards were falling all around them. Hot blazes were coming from under the floor as windowpanes exploded, sending glass particles flying in all directions.

After moving clear of the rooming house, the man showed no mercy as he tossed Elly onto an open wagon bed. "Stay put, or so help me, I will hit you," he yelled over his shoulder.

Elly sat up in the wagon bed. Pushing her hair out of her smoke-filled eyes, she felt chilled to the bone. Realizing that she was wearing only a thin housecoat, a shift, and her bloomers, she pulled her mama's quilt tight around her shoulders.

Mrs. Duffy, a sixty-something woman, raced over to Elly and threw her arms around her. "Oh dear, it looks like we're homeless," she cried. "Everything I owned was in that rooming house. I scrambled to save a few things, but the back of the house was first to go. All the pretty things my dear Homer had given me, all gone up in smoke."

Mrs. Duffy plopped a large tin container on the edge of the wagon bed and wrapped her arms around it. "At least I remembered to get my money box," she said to Elly. "I can start fresh somewhere else, but oh Lord, where?"

"I remembered my money too, but my dear brother beat me to it. It's all gone, thanks to him." Elly pulled her knees up under her chin and wrapped her arms around them. *Can anything else possibly go wrong?*

"Oh, dear." Mrs. Duffy sighed. She wondered if she should be the bearer of bad news to her tenant and friend or not say a word. Elly had being living in her rooming house for two years after the owner of her little house placed it up for sale. Elly had made her younger brother get out and support himself. Taking a big breath, she decided that Elly should know about her brother.

"Elly," Mrs. Duffy hesitated, then said, "a scuffle out in the street woke me up a little while ago, before the fire. A bunch of men had a rope tied around a young man's neck and they were screaming that if he ever showed his face in town again, they would hang him for sure. The sheriff threatened him with jail time. I heard him call the boy Tim. I'm sure it was Timmy."

Elly's shocked expression was almost too much for Mrs. Duffy. "Maybe I shouldn't have told you about him. I'm so sorry to add to your troubles."

"Oh, Mrs. Duffy, you know Timmy and the trouble I've had with him. He never wanted to help me or take on any responsibility. Maybe in another town, he'll get a fresh start. I have enough trouble of my own now to be worrying about him." Sighing, Elly said, "I spoiled him too much."

"But he's your brother and he wasn't bad—maybe spoiled, like you said—but he helped me a lot around the rooming house most of the time, whenever I asked him. Aren't you afraid you won't ever see him again?"

"Timmy loves me, just like I love him," she said laughing a little. "He'll show up wherever I am." Leaning her back against the wagon, she gazed up at the stars.

***

"I see you have found something to laugh about in this awful situation," said the big brute of a man who had rescued her from the burning building.

Elly was embarrassed the tall cowboy had seen her in her state of undress. He'd saved her from the burning building by manhandling her like a sack of grain. Well, he wouldn't see her that way again. She pulled her mama's quilt tight. "No, there's nothing funny about being left homeless or penniless," Elly said, as she lowered her legs and tucked the quilt around them.

"Mrs. Duffy," the young man tipped his hat to the landlady. "I guess I won't be needing the room. I'll stay the night at the wagon train."

"Oh, Mr. Maynard. I'm so sorry. I have no idea where I'm going to stay or Miss Eddy either. Have you seen the preacher? Maybe he might have a suggestion as to where we can spend the night," Mrs. Duffy said.

"The few buildings that let rooms are pretty much burned down, except some upstairs rooms at Wild Bill's place. The fire that started in the back of the bakery spread like wildfire jumping from one rooftop to another. The men were able to wet down a few of the buildings to stop the fire," explained the young Mr. Maynard, glancing down at his damp, smoky clothes. "The major and I have a few covered wagons parked on the outskirts of town if you and the Missus would like to rest in one of them tonight. They're clean and have fresh blankets and quilts in them."

"What do you think, Elly?" Mrs. Duffy asked. "Just for one night until we can find another place."

"How much?" whispered Elly. "I told you I have no funds."

"The lodging for the night is free, Miss," Tate Maynard snapped. "Come on. I'll take you two down to the wagons."

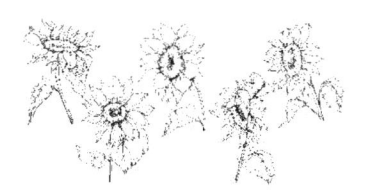

Chapter 3

Major Charles Maynard, a handsome man with salt and pepper hair, rose when his son drove the flatbed into the circle of his wagon train. "Howdy, son," Major sauntered to the lead horse and took the reins to settle the frightened animal down. "Have all the fires been put out?" Major asked Tate. "The whole town looked like it was on fire."

"Yep, but the bakery and the boardinghouse, part of the schoolhouse, and the roof of the church have been destroyed. Everything else is pretty much filled with smoke, but at least they're standing. Mrs. Duffy and the schoolteacher, who had been living at her rooming house, have been left stranded tonight. I've offered one of our new wagons for them to stay the night. I was sure you wouldn't mind."

Major walked to the back of the wagon and offered a hand to Mrs. Duffy to help her off the wagon. "Sorry to hear about your boarding place. It's been part of this town for years. Maybe you can rebuild." He offered to help Elly down, but she slid off the back of the wagon, trying to cover her body with the quilt at the same time.

"I don't know, Mr. Maynard," replied Mrs. Duffy. "I'm thinking about taking what little I have and moving somewhere else. Maybe get a fresh start away from Wild Bill's. I'd like a quieter place at the edge of a town where my boarders won't have to worry every time they walk out of their rooms onto the busy street."

"Maybe you should consider signing up with me and travel to Sunflower, Texas. I'm going to leave next week with a train full of mail-order brides. I'd be happy to have you travel with us."

When Mrs. Duffy didn't respond, he turned to his son. "Tate, take these nice ladies to the first wagon in the circle. They'll be safe there tonight." Major slapped Tate on the back and walked toward the bonfire where several men sat drinking coffee.

Tate drove the wagon about twenty yards, then stopped. He leaped down from the wagon seat and walked toward the two ladies that trailed the wagon.

"Mrs. Duffy, do you have a carpetbag of items like the missy?"

"Afraid not, sir. I have my life savings in this tin box," she whispered for his ears only, "and the old rocking chair that my husband built for me. I dragged it out the back door and left it standing in the back yard. Come morning, I'll go and get it. I can purchase myself a few pieces of clothing if the dry-goods store is still standing."

Tate smiled at the older woman's spirit and turned to take Elly's carpetbag and place it in the covered wagon. "I'm not helpless, sir. You have helped me enough by packing me a bag full of my personal items." Her face reddened and she looked away.

"I didn't pack anything for you, Miss. I placed you over my shoulder and grabbed your carpetbag by the door. You must have packed earlier."

"What? I never packed anything. You didn't give me time," Elly said, her voice rising with every word.

Mrs. Duffy stepped between them and said, "Mr. Maynard, you may help me up into the wagon. I'm exhausted and ready to turn in for the evening."

"Be happy to help you. Would you like a pail of warm water to have in the wagon? I can get it for you."

"She may not, but I would. If it isn't too much trouble," Elly responded. "I'd like to wash off some of the smoke and ashes."

Elly climbed into the covered wagon with Mrs. Duffy and was surprised at how nice it was. It was much larger than it appeared from the outside. There were two beds, one on each side, with clean quilts, and pillows placed at one end. The space between the beds was ample enough for two people to pass. Under the beds were built-in drawers for storage and overhead there were hooks of various sizes to hang supplies.

"Ladies, here's the water you requested," said Tate. "Just yell out if you get frightened. Major and I are in the next wagon. Good night."

Elly reached through the opening in the back of the wagon and took the bucket of water and two fresh towels. "Thank you, and good night," she replied and quickly tied the end of the covered wagon closed.

Mrs. Duffy had fallen asleep while waiting for Mr. Maynard to bring them the pail of warm water. Elly rinsed her face and hands clean. A soft snore came from the older woman. This had been a stressful evening for both of them. Dipping the end of one of the towels into the water, Elly used it as a washcloth. She removed her robe and sprinkled the water over her smoke-smudged skin. Taking her hairbrush, Elly gave her hair a thorough brushing to remove the ashes and dust. Afterward, feeling as clean as possible, she lay down on the wagon bed and covered herself with her mama's quilt. She was too tired to cry over all the things she lost in the fire. Mrs. Duffy's light snoring soothed her nerves as she drifted off to sleep.

Chapter 4

Laughter and horseplay around the campfire woke Elly from a deep sleep. Mrs. Duffy's bed was empty. Pushing the quilt down to the end of the bed and putting her bare feet on the floor, Elly listened to the conversation coming from outside and heard Mrs. Duffy's soft laughter. The older woman was an early riser, so naturally she'd be up and ready for the new day.

Elly needed to dress and go check on the damage of the rooming house and schoolhouse. She also needed to check on her friend, Ruby, and see how the fire affected the saloon. Ruby wanted to travel on the wagon train, so maybe this would be her opportunity to leave this town.

Elly needed to purchase some clothes, but how? With all her funds gone and another week until payday, it was going to be nearly impossible to replace much-needed items.

The carpetbag that the cowboy had taken from her room was sitting inside the opening at the front of the wagon. She reached over and opened it. The bag belonged to Timmy, of course. Pulling items out of it, she saw that it contained clothes, a few decks of cards, a razor, toothbrush and paste, and a worn wallet that held one dirty dollar bill. *One dollar.* Since it was old and worn, it must have a special meaning to him. Well, it was hers now, and she would use it if needed.

Elly couldn't go about town in just a robe covering her underclothes, so she took a pair of Timmy's blue jeans and a long-sleeved shirt and put them on. The clothes were a perfect fit for her slim body. Of course, the townspeople would be scandalized to see her dressed in men's clothes, but they would have to understand that she had no choice today.

After she dressed and pinned her hair up into a twist, she climbed down from the wagon and landed on the ground with bare feet. Another problem to deal with, Elly thought. No shoes or boots.

"Well, good morning, dear," Mrs. Duffy said from her seat on a log near the fire. She was holding a cup of hot coffee and eating a delicious-looking biscuit.

All the men who were sitting around the fire jumped up, and with wide eyes, nodded their morning greeting. "Good morning, Miss," Major Maynard spoke first. "Have a seat, and I will bring you a cup of hot coffee. Would you like a little sugar and cream?"

"Yes, please. Just a little," Elly said as she glanced around at the men who were wondering why she was dressed in men's clothes. Tate Maynard was nowhere in sight.

As Major handed her the cup of coffee, she said, "Please forgive my attire this morning. The carpetbag that was saved from my room belonged to my brother, so all I have to wear is his clothes. Thank goodness we're about the same size," she said.

"You looked just fine, Missy." Major glanced down at her bare feet. "I guess your brother didn't have an extra pair of boots in his bag?"

"You're right about that. I was so confused and scared I only grabbed my hairbrush, my Bible and a quilt that my mama had made years ago."

"Don't fret, Elly. I'll walk downtown and purchase you a pair of shoes. You should eat one of Mr. Henry's biscuits. They're divine," Mrs. Duffy said with a twinkle in her eye.

"I will, but Mrs. Duffy, I can't allow you to spend your money on me." The older woman was going to need all of her money to get settled in another town.

"We'll call it a loan, dearie, if that makes you feel better," she replied with a sweet smile. "When I return, you can go and check out the schoolhouse and see when you can begin classes again."

"Yes, I will need to do that, but I know they aren't going to allow me to teach in men's clothes. I may be able to borrow a dress or two from some of the ladies in town," Elly said, wondering what kind of handouts she would be given to wear. Maybe the owner of the dry-goods store would give her credit to purchase a ready-made dress until she got paid. Her spirits lifted a little as she remembered seeing some dresses in his window last week.

After Mrs. Duffy returned from town with a sturdy pair of short brown ankle boots, Elly dusted the seat of her trousers. "I'm going to have a look at the schoolhouse and try to meet with Mr. Roberts, the school superintendent, about when school will reopen."

A booming voice from behind her caused her to nearly jump out of her skin. "Where in hades do you think you're going, dressed in men's clothes? No respectable lady parades her fanny downtown dressed like that."

Elly pulled herself straight and tall and glared at young Mr. Maynard. "Shall I wear the only ladies clothes that I own down the middle of Main Street? Do you think a thin white shift and bloomers covering my body would be better, sir?"

Tate Maynard, well over six feet in height and shoulders broad as a barn door, stood a foot away from Elly with his wide hands braced on his low-slung gun belt. "Well, of course not, but you aren't decent in the outfit you have on."

"Oh, son, everybody will understand that she has lost all of her personal items in the fire. She's got to go and check on her job and see about getting a dress or two." Major Maynard tried to contain his laughter at his son's attitude.

"I understand she has business to take care of, but she'll

probably cause a riot walking down the street . . . like that."

Major stood and tossed his remaining coffee into the fire. "Tell you what, son. You go with her and make sure she's not pestered by any of the men in town." Major gave Tate a little nudge.

"That's best, I suppose," Tate said and gave Elly the once-over again.

"Now you listen to me, Mister. Just because you allowed me to stay in your wagon last night does not give you cause to think you can control what I do and when I do it. You got that?" Elly whirled around and marched down the dirt path that led to Main Street.

"Go on and watch after her, Mr. Maynard," Mrs. Duffy called as she sat and drank her second cup of coffee. Her eyes twinkled.

"Mule-headed woman," Tate mumbled, stepping up his pace to catch up with Elly. Just as Tate had predicted, men started whistling and making sounds like a howling dog or a big cat. Some even invited her to come and sit on their laps. With a sharp glance from Tate, the remarks ceased.

Elly seemed to be ignoring the whistles and catcalls of the men around her. She started toward Wild Bill's Saloon when Tate grabbed her elbow and stopped her. "Where do you think you're going? You can't go in that place."

"I need to check on my friend who lives upstairs." Elly said as she peered up at the windows on the second floor of the building. "This place didn't burn like the other buildings, did it?" she asked Tate. "Maybe you can go inside and ask about her . . . for me."

"Damn," he swore. "What's the gal's name?" He didn't care for this particular saloon and he sure didn't like going inside to search for one of the young ladies that worked there. His name would be linked with hers for months on end.

"Ruby Jackson. She wants to travel on your wagon train and get out of this town. Maybe this will be her chance."

"Now, hold on right there," Tate said. This was too much for anyone to ask of him. "I'm not taking whores on my wagon train as brides for my future grooms. I'll check on her, but if she wants to leave town, it won't be with me." Tate marched through the swinging doors and disappeared into the dark, smoky building.

Elly was so mad she could spit, but she stood on the boardwalk waiting for Mr. Boss Man's return when suddenly, Ruby came hurrying from up the street. "Elly, Elly, here I am. I've been so worried about you. Gracious, why are you dressed in men's clothes?" Ruby took both of Elly's hands in hers.

"I'm fine, except I lost everything in the fire. All my clothes and personal items. Timmy stole my money, but that's another story. How are you and the other girls doing?"

"Oh, we're all fine. Listen," she said softly, "I told Bill that I was making plans to leave on the wagon train, and he said if I did, he would have me arrested. I owe him money and I have to work it off. If I try to sneak away, he'll send men after me. Looks like I'm stuck here for a while," she said, wiping her eyes with a clean hanky.

Tate reappeared at Elly's side. Ruby was still standing on the boardwalk holding Elly's hand. He stood listening to the girl's sad conversation.

"I heard that you might have to leave town to get another teaching job. I'll sure miss you if you leave." Ruby grabbed Elly around the waist, gave her a quick hug, the raced into the saloon.

"It's a shame that a person can nearly own another person like that Wild Bill does the women who work for him. You don't have to worry about Ruby asking to go on your wagon train. Wild Bill will have her arrested if she leaves town." Elly said and looked up at him with narrowed eyes.

"Hey, now look here. I have no control over those girls that work in that saloon any more than you do. They chose to work there. You had to support yourself, but you chose to work hard with your hands—not on your back."

Elly couldn't believe the vulgar words that came out of Tate's mouth. His words were crude and downright mean. Her face flamed a bright red, and she was so angry she couldn't do anything but sputter. She glared at him and stormed down the street ahead of him.

Just as Elly reached the gate that led to the schoolyard, Tate reached in front of her and grabbed her hand. "You can't go any further than this. It's too dangerous," he said, pointing to the roof and one side of the building that was leaning.

"Oh my." Elly's hand covered her mouth. "There's no way this building will be repaired in a week or two. It will probably have to be torn down and rebuilt."

"That's true. The town will have to hold school in some other building, or not at all," replied Tate.

"That's what I'm afraid of. I'm out of a job as of today. There's no other building or barn nearby that can be used as a classroom with so many students."

As Elly and Tate were preparing to leave the area, Mr. Roberts, the school superintendent, and Mrs. Turnberry, a member of the school board, approached. "Well, Miss Eddy, it looks to me like this is the final straw. I can't believe that you would be out in public dressed in that . . . outfit. Don't you have any self-respect?" Mrs. Turnberry asked with a scowl on her face. The old woman demanded that Mr. Roberts cancel Elly's school contract.

"Miss Eddy, I know you have a good explanation for your attire, but you have a reputation to uphold, and to be an example of what and how a lady behaves in public. I wouldn't be a bit surprised if you didn't have something to do with burning the school down. Since you began teaching for us, you have never endeavored to act in accordance with our standards for a teacher. Now, here you are parading downtown in men's attire. What's next?" He yelled as he wiped the sweat off his forehead and around his mouth. "We will not be renewing your contract for the coming year. Good day."

The two upstanding citizens of Leesville marched up the street with their heads close together. Elly stared after them, speechless.

Tate Maynard stood still, his hands into fists. He couldn't believe what had just taken place. He knew people would be shocked by Elly's trousers, but those two old goats didn't allow her the opportunity to explain why she was dressed in men's clothes. Surely, they knew that she lived at the rooming house and it had burned to the ground. And that remark about her being responsible for setting the town on fire. Why would he say such a thing?

"Come on. Let's go to the dry goods store and buy you a dress to wear. After you're out of these clothes you're wearing, you can go and try to reason with Mr. Roberts alone."

Elly said nothing as she followed Tate down the boardwalk to the dry goods store. They were met by the owner, Mr. Thomason, his skinny arms folded across his chest and his bony chin in the air as he looked down at the young couple.

"How can I help you today, Mr. Maynard?" he asked without even acknowledging Elly's presence.

"I don't need any more supplies at this time, but Miss Eddy needs a ready-made dress. Can you help her?" Mr. Thomason made no comment, but his eyes traveled from her black hair to her dusty boots.

Before the store owner could respond, Elly spoke up, "Mr. Thomason, I'm afraid that I have no funds until the school board pays me next week. Will you give me credit until I receive my pay?"

"No," he replied. He circled behind the counter to check out another customer who was waiting.

Tate Maynard could not believe his ears. He was sure he had

misunderstood Mr. Thomason, and he didn't care for the rudeness the shopkeeper displayed to Miss Eddy. After the customer had completed his business with Mr. Thomason, Tate stepped up close to the tall man. "Now, Mr. Thomason, this lady needs to purchase a dress so she will have something decent to wear. You do know that all of her clothes were burned in the fire last night?"

"Yep, I know. I also know that the school board is not going to pay Miss Eddy any money for the past month. I overheard them discussing her behavior and how she had broken part of her contract. So no money, no credit. Now excuse me, Mr. Maynard. I have work to do."

The old man disappeared through a curtain. Conversation over.

Elly was standing at the counter with disbelief written across her face. "The school board is not going to pay me my salary for this month because I broke my contract?" She spun around to walk out of the store onto the old wooden gray boardwalk. "I broke my contract," Elly mumbled. "I can't believe they're holding the fire against me. It's like I burned all my clothes so I could wear my brother's pants—" Elly lowered her eyes. To say she was surprised about the decision would be an understatement. She was lost for a comment.

"Listen, Miss Eddy. Major will speak with the mayor. He will get your money. Let's go back to the wagons and tell him what's taken place." On their walk back, Tate finally asked, "Why would Mr. Roberts accuse you of starting the town fire?"

"Oh, he thinks I'm a jinx," she replied.

Chapter 5

"Now Mr. Maynard," Mr. Roberts cleared his throat and continued with his explanation about Miss Eddy and her salary for the past month. "This young teacher has been with us for two years, and she has never performed in the lady-like manner that we have expected of her. You can't imagine all the problems she has caused the school board. Her first winter, she nearly burned the school down. She cooked a dish in her classroom and fed it to the children. Nearly poisoned them all. The list goes on and on. After that first year, we were divided as to renewing her contract, but the men on the committee felt sorry for her and wanted to give her another chance."

"Those sound like things that could happen to anyone. What other things has she done to make you want to dismiss her?"

"What hasn't she done would be a better question. One night, she marched into Wild Bill's Saloon and dragged her screaming young brother, who was playing cards, out into the street. He caused an awful ruckus because he had a winning hand. Lately, she has befriended a little whore who works at Wild Bill's. She ushers her all over town with their arms linked together—even brought her into the bakery to have tea. When she's been asked to leave, she makes a scene when she exits. The older boy students dislike her to the point that she can't teach them. She's always trying to make them stay after school, but they're afraid of her. They think she may be a witch."

"Good gracious, old man. You can't possibly believe something like that," Major said.

"I don't make judgments, but the ladies on the committee are upset. Since her mama died, Miss Eddy has been a different person. Like I said, she has not set a good example for our young students. Therefore, we have advertised for a new male teacher to replace her."

"I think that's fine, but none of the things you have said are reasons for not giving Miss Eddy her salary. You'd have continued to allow her to teach until the end of her contract if the fire had not taken place."

"Well, I guess. But she has broken her contract, which gives us reason not to have to pay her. I'm sorry, Mr. Maynard. She'll not receive one dime for teaching this past month, and her contract will not be renewed. Good day, sir." Mr. Roberts sat down at his desk and picked up papers that seemed more important than continuing his conversation with Major Maynard.

As Major stood, he tapped his big Stetson on his right leg and glared down at Mr. Roberts. As he turned to leave, Mr. Roberts made a comment, "Why don't you sign Miss Eddy up to become one of your mail-order brides? Take her away from Leesville, and get her a man that can make her toe the line and act like a lady."

"That may be the smartest thing you've said all morning. Good day to you." Major slapped his hat on his head and stormed out of the office.

Angry at the superintendent's words, Major strode back to the dry goods store. He glanced around until he saw what he was looking for. He walked over to the rack of ready-made dresses and selected a blue calico. Slinging the dress over his shoulder, he continued to the back of the store that held all types of material and other notions that ladies used.

"Can I help you, Mr.," asked a young girl whom Major had

never seen in the store before.

"Yes, I want the makings for a young lady's underthings. You know what I mean," he said as he ran a hand up and down his shoulders to his waist, then brushed his pant legs to make sure she understood he needed bloomer things, too. "Choose everything she will need. She's about your size."

Blushing bright red, the young lady nodded and began to select yards of white muslin, white thread, pearl buttons, soft cotton lace and stays. After cutting the material, she wrapped all the items in brown paper and gave Mr. Thomason, the store owner, a piece of paper with the items listed on it.

Major Maynard tucked the package under his arm and hurried out of the store. As he neared the wagon train, he saw a group of young ladies surrounded by carpetbags and trunks. He hated this part of the trip. The men in Sunflower, Texas, were waiting on decent girls to become their brides, and it was up to him to decide which ones were fit to make the trip.

As he neared the wagon with a tent placed next to it, he called to Eleanor Eddy to follow him. She glanced over her shoulder at Mrs. Duffy, then headed to where Mr. Maynard had motioned.

He stopped walking and spun around. "Before I forget, here is a dress for you and some material to make yourself some other things. Don't thank me now. I have a plan, and if you agree, you can earn money and you would be a big help to me and Tate."

Before she could ask him any questions about this plan, he pushed over a stool and asked her to sit. "Look, Miss Eddy. You being an educated woman can help me with signing those ladies up to make the trip across Texas to become brides. Many of the girls won't be right for the trip, and it's darn hard for Tate and me to tell them they can't travel with us."

Major smiled at her. "I would like for you to talk to the ladies, ask them personal questions, and get other important information you think we should know about them. You will have to record their names and all the other necessaries. This is difficult for us to handle too."

Elly remained quiet. She watched Mr. Maynard with his big, fidgeting hands.

"It's like this. You need to relocate to another town if you want to teach school again. We're traveling to Sunflower, Texas, and it's going to be a hard trip. You can start a new life. Sunflower's a quiet town that has many stores, a schoolhouse, a small church, and even a bank. I wouldn't ask you to travel to this town if it wasn't a nice place. In fact, Tate and I own several hundred acres and a nice ranch house there. This will be our last trip because we plan to settle there and raise cattle."

Elly started to ask a question, but he held up his hand for her to wait.

"But, getting back to the job offer. You'll help us keep the ladies in line and teach them all the things they'll have to learn. The girls are going to have to drive their own wagons, haul water, and care for their team. Everyone will take a turn helping out in the chuck wagon. Before we leave, they will all have to learn to shoot a gun. We'll only have a few men traveling with us who mostly care for the extra animals during the day. Many of the women will want to carry too many items with them. The wagons and teams can only carry so much, so you'll instruct them about what they can bring. This is probably the hardest part of their leaving."

"May I speak now, Mr. Maynard?" Elly asked, trying not to laugh at his expression. "First, I thank you for the clothes. It was nice of you to purchase the items for me. I really haven't planned to leave this town, but it looks like I'm not wanted here any longer. My brother Timmy is not welcome here either." Elly gave a big sigh. "He's already left."

Elly glanced over to the wagon where Mrs. Duffy was sitting. "I'll go with you if Mrs. Duffy will come along. She would be able to help with the ladies. As far as teaching the women to handle the animals, I've never driven a team. I did when I was a child and lived at home, but that's been years. I've never shot a gun in my life so I can't teach them to do that. Maybe I'm not the woman you need for this job."

"Miss Eddy, you are the perfect person for the job I have laid out." Major watched the young ladies form a line near the chuck wagon.

"The men will help instruct the ladies on how to care for the animals and how to shoot. It's all the other little problems that pop up along the trail that drive me crazy. You'll be the one who answers their questions and keeps peace in the group. The ladies get tired and snappy. Before you know it, we'll have a cat fight, and the ladies are at each other throats the whole way. I hate that," he said, his hands balling up into fists. "I've wanted to paddle a few of them, but I can't do that."

Trying hard not to laugh at Mr. Maynard as he described other things that took place between the women, Elly had to look away. "I believe I understand what you're saying," she replied. "You want me to sign up the ladies, take all their personal information, find out what they're expecting in their husbands-to-be and tell them what is expected of them. If they can't agree to help on the trail, then they cannot be a mail-order bride, correct?"

"That's right. By George, I believe you and I will work great together, Miss Eddy."

"Mr. Maynard, if we're going to work together, you may call me Elly, short for Eleanor." She grinned at him and picked up the brown package he had given her before they began their discussion.

"Elly, you may call me Major, but when addressing me in front of the ladies, then call me Mr. Maynard, please."

"Oh, Major. One serious question. What will your son have to say about me joining forces with you on this trip?"

"You do your job and he will be thrilled you're traveling with us. The women drive him crazy, so he stays out on the trail until dark most days." Major looked over his shoulder, then motioned that the ladies were already lining up. "Good luck, Elly."

Chapter 6

After a long afternoon of taking down the brides' information, Elly and Mrs. Duffy sat in the assigned covered wagon that would be their new home for the next two months. Elly took the brown package and untied the twine. The ready-made dress was lying on top. Elly shook the dress out and laid it across her lap. "Oh, my goodness. This is so pretty," she said.

Mrs. Duffy picked up some tiny pearl buttons and a long piece of lace. "Look at all these things. Someone knew what they were doing. The muslin is so soft and will make great underclothes. There's enough material for several sets, not just one."

"Mrs. Duffy, Mr. Maynard meant for you to use some of these things. This can't be all for me," Elly responded.

"No, this is all for you. I have money to buy new things already made. This is part of your payment for helping with the women on the train."

"Are you sure? I hate to go ask him because he acted embarrassed just giving me the package." Elly laughed as she remembered Major's expression.

"Yes, I'm sure. Look at this. A new pair of scissors has been included. We can lay out the material on one of our beds and use your old bloomers as a pattern. We can use my corset as a pattern too."

Later, after cutting out her new undies, Elly needed to stretch and use her legs. Mrs. Duffy had fallen asleep on her bed for a much-needed nap.

Elly strolled over to the chuck wagon and met Henry, the cook for the wagon train.

"Howdy, Miss, I'm Henry," he said with a grin behind his handlebar mustache. His eyes were as blue as a stream of crystal water.

"Howdy yourself. My name is Eleanor Eddy, but you can call me Elly, since I will be traveling with you."

"So, you're headed to Sunflower looking for a new husband? A gal as pretty as you shouldn't have to be a mail-order bride."

"Thank you for the compliment, I think." She smiled at the older man. "But I'm not going to be one of the new brides. I'll be assisting Mr. Maynard with the women and all their needs. He mentioned that the ladies will be taking turns helping you in the chuck wagon. What will you be expecting them to do for you?"

"Well, I always need someone to help me keep hot water on the fire, a gal to keep the coffee pot full, and someone to wash the dishes. Is that what you mean?"

"Yes, what you have suggested are important duties. At every mealtime, you will need at least three women to help you. May I ask—if the ladies can cook, would you allow them to help you prepare things like soups, stews, biscuits, or fried pies?"

"Shoot fire, girl. If you can find me someone who can cook like that, I'll be their helper." Henry grinned from ear to ear as he fingered his mustache.

"Several of the ladies that signed on this morning said they loved to cook. We should allow those ladies to help. This will keep them from being bored on this long trip. When we stop close to towns, they can supply you with a list of fresh vegetables, and dried or fresh fruits that will be needed. I will ask Major what he thinks about the idea."

"No need to bother him. I'm in charge of feeding the trail hands and everyone else. You just send me some of those great cooks, and everyone will be happy. Especially Major, who loves good food."

"Do you need help this evening?" Elly asked. "I can cook or wash dishes. Whatever you need me to do because I'm restless. So can I peel potatoes, carrots, or do whatever needs to be done to help?"

"Sure thing. Grab yourself an apron hanging just inside the wagon there, and I'll get you some spuds to peel. I have beef stew cooking, but the fellows like to pile some on top of mashed 'taters."

Elly secured the big white apron around her small waist. The apron draped around her like a skirt and hid her trousers. As she sat on a barrel, Henry entertained her with stories about other trips he had taken with Major and Tate.

As the sun slowly set, the men gathered around. She watched a few of them feed the oxen, mules and workhorses. They corralled all the animals into one large pen. One of the men picked up a guitar and began playing.

Henry poured hot water in several shallow pans for the men to use to wash up. Clean hand towels lay at the end of the bench. Henry rang the dinner bell.

The men lined up and seemed surprised to have Elly serve them as they passed their plates. She piled mashed potatoes on their plate and topped them with the hearty beef stew that contained small potatoes, carrots, and wild onions. She placed two large biscuits on each plate and received a big smile from every man. At the end of the table, Henry served hot coffee.

Major held out his plate to Elly. She spooned him an extra helping of mashed potatoes and covered them with the stew. A grin spread across his face as she placed three large biscuits on the plate.

"You're a fine woman," he said and carried his plate over to his makeshift table and barrel.

Elly served Henry his plate and prepared Mrs. Duffy and herself one. Tate was not present for dinner, so she fixed an extra-large plate and covered it with a clean dishcloth in case he came in later. The men were allowed to have seconds after everyone had been served.

Later in the evening, Elly was relaxing on a log near her wagon. She was making a list of her concerns for the women she had signed to become mail-order brides. At the top of her list was the word, 'boredom.'

"Why aren't you tucked in your bed like Mrs. Duffy?" a voice came from the dark that she recognized as Tate's.

"Oh, Mr. Maynard, you made me jump," she said as she laid her hand over her heart. "I could ask you how come you're so late coming in for supper, but you're a grown man and can come and go as you like."

Tate gave a laugh and he glanced at her. "Glad you view me that way. I wish Major would remember that I'm a big boy."

"Being his only son, he worries about you, I'm sure," replied Elly.

"You're probably right. What are you writing there?" he said, pointing to her pad.

"Your pa has put me in charge of keeping the brides-to-be happy on this trip. My biggest concern for them is boredom. Oh, they'll be tired at first from driving the wagons, helping with the cooking, collecting firewood and keeping the fires burning. After a while, they will get used to the work, and then they'll become bored. Women tend to get irritated and short-tempered when they're just sitting around, just like children."

"On every trip we have a catfight, and the ladies have to be separated. I get so tired of threatening the women. If it were up to me, I'd let them fight it out." Tate must have noted Elly's shocked expression. "What ideas do you have that will keep the ladies on their best behavior?"

"I noticed that some of the women couldn't read and had to sign the contract with an 'x.' Most of them have had little schooling, but when I asked if they would like to learn to read and write, they readily agreed. So, I was thinking about holding classes during the day and after supper when we stop and rest. While some of the ladies are driving the wagons, others can read or practice writing, if I have supplies to give them."

"Where will you get books? I have a few, but they're not for a beginner."

"I've been sitting here pondering an idea." Elly said, then jumped off the log. "If I could get into the schoolhouse, I could gather my books that might not have been burned or damaged. I had several first and second grade readers in my desk and some slates that they could use to write on." Elly's eyebrows rose. "Oh, I saved some dinner for you. I know you must be hungry," she said sweetly, as she prepared to walk to the chuck wagon and get his plate.

"All right. Hold it right there. You're trying hard to soften me up. What do you want me to do? Not that I'm agreeing to do anything."

Elly turned to face him. "Would you please agree to come with me? We can slip into the school building and get some supplies that belong to me. That way, I can teach the ladies." Elly explained, her voice rising.

Tate looked at the lovely schoolteacher and then glanced at the other wagons. He was going to have to be careful around this girl or he'd be the first in the marriage line in Sunflower. "You do have a good plan, but you can't walk downtown looking like that." He stood for a second and then said, "It's late, so we probably won't meet up with anyone on the boardwalk. You'll need to wear a hat on your head and wrap that rope of hair under it."

Elly followed Tate to his wagon while he reached into the back and pulled out a black cowboy hat that fit down over her ears. "That's a good look for you. A person can't see your lovely hair or your pretty eyes," then realized what came out of his mouth. "If we meet someone, just keep your head down and don't speak. Let me do all the talking."

As Tate and Elly hurried down the boardwalk toward the schoolhouse, they didn't notice they were being watched by a drifter and his partner who kept to the shadows. He had recognized Tate as being the owner of the big wagon train—a good prospect to rob.

Tate held open the gate to the schoolhouse, warning Elly to be careful where she stepped. The building still had two sides standing, but the roof was nearly ready to collapse. As they approached the opening of one wall, Elly was thrilled to see her desk was just as she had left it on Friday. She picked up a crate and carried it over to her desk, then from the bottom drawer, she gathered a handful of readers that would be helpful in teaching the brides. *Oh, this is a wonderful idea.*

The next drawer contained writing paper and pencils that she'd loaned to students, a big box of chalk and three slates that were for new students. On top of her desk was an unopened inkwell and several ink pens. She placed them carefully in the crate.

Elly glanced around the room and whispered to Tate, "Let's look in the students' desks and remove their slates and anything else that could be used in my makeshift classroom."

"I thought we came after a few books. We're taking everything that isn't tied down," he said frowning at her. "We could be arrested for stealing."

"No, I'm not stealing. They owe me money for teaching school this past month. I'm getting my payment by taking school supplies they're going to replace anyway." She surveyed the burned building that looked as if the side wall might cave in with a hard wind.

"I'm ready," she said and tried to pick up the crate.

"Here, I've got that. Let's go, but let's be careful leaving. We don't want to be seen with this crate of supplies." Tate opened the gate that led onto the boardwalk and glanced both ways. Seeing no one out this time of night, he took Elly's arm.

As the young couple whispered and laughed about their useful treasure, Elly saw a movement behind them. A gun was rammed hard into Tate's back. A man with foul-smelling breath demanded that he put the crate on the ground and empty his pockets. The man's partner reached for Elly's hat, and her long hair fell down her back. The man immediately flopped Elly's hat on his own head, and grinned widely.

"Look here, Billy Joe. This guy's got tits! He ain't no man at all. He's a gal."

"Shut your trap, stupid fool. Why don't you just go ring the school bell and call the sheriff to come and get us?"

Tate dug into his pockets and pulled out a few dollars and a handful of coins as the nasty man reached out and touched Elly's chest again. She slapped the dumb man's face so hard his head spun, and he bumped into Tate causing him to drop the money onto the boardwalk.

"Stop playing around and help me gather up this man's money." The drifter scrambled to the ground to pick up the money while still holding Tate at gunpoint.

"You shouldn't have done that," snarled the young man to Elly. "Now, I'm going to have to shoot you."

"Go ahead and shoot because if you touch me again, I'll claw your eyes out."

"You gotta say you're sorry and give me a kiss and I won't shoot you."

Before Elly could reply, the dirty man pulled her into his arms.

Elly pushed herself back away from the man's chest, then grabbed him by his hair and pulled his head toward her face. She clamped down on his right ear. Blood spewed everywhere as he screamed louder than a Comanche. He shoved her away and ran off into the shadows holding the side of his head. As the drifter glanced up at the fight between his partner and Elly, Tate rammed his knee into the man's face, busting his nose while knocking him flat on his back, unconscious.

Tate grabbed the crate with one hand and Elly's arm with his other and dragged her down the boardwalk. After they reached the clearing where the wagons were parked, they stopped running. Elly rubbed a cramp in her left side, then started laughing. Tate gazed at the young schoolteacher's face, speckled with blood and her hair hanging wild about her shoulders. Suddenly, he was laughing, too.

"I'm so sorry . . . that you . . . got robbed, Mr. Maynard," Elly said, holding her stomach.

"Don't be," he replied and bent over to catch his breath. "I only dropped a few dollars and some coins. They were desperate for money or couldn't count. The sidekick was determined to pick up every coin off the ground."

"I know. He never knew what hit him when you knee him. I think you broke his nose because blood was everywhere. Thank goodness we got away from them," Elly said.

"You're right. I'm glad I never had to pull my gun on them." Tate's eyes traveled from her head to her toes. "I'm just making sure you're not hurt."

"Well, it's late and we had better turn in." Elly said, feeling a bit uncomfortable as Tate inspected her body with his eyes.

"Let me place this heavy crate under your wagon tonight, and you can sort the things out tomorrow. You're going to have to wash the blood off your face," he said with a big grin. "Well, good night, Miss Eddy.

"Please call me Elly," she said softly.

"Only if you call me Tate," he responded.

She walked to the back of her wagon, secretly smiling.

Chapter 7

Early the next day, after Elly and Mrs. Duffy helped Henry with breakfast, the new brides-to-be arrived with their prized possessions. Elly remembered what Major had said earlier about the ladies and their belongings. She also knew how her first order of business would be received by the women. They would hate her.

The women found places to stand. It was then that Elly noticed a child, a little boy about five, sitting on a big box beside one of the young women. Mr. Maynard hadn't mentioned that the women could bring children.

Taking a deep breath, Elly strolled over to the young girl. She remembered her name was Mattie Mathews. "Good morning, Mattie," Elly said and smiled at the child who hid behind Mattie's dress.

"Morning, ma'am," the young lady replied as she stepped in front of the boy.

"Please call me Miss Eddy for now," Elly replied, thinking that the ladies needed to see her as someone in charge.

"Yes, ma'am," Mattie said, holding the child back with her hand.

"Who do you have with you this morning?" Elly peered around the girl's full skirt.

"This here's my little brother, Johnny," she said and pulled the child to stand in front of her. "I've taken care of him since our folks died. He has no one but me, and I can't leave him behind. I've just got to take him with me or the sheriff will place in him in one of those homes that will work him to death—" The girl's voice quivered and became louder with every word.

"Now, Mattie. This is my first trip on the wagon train, and I have been placed in charge of the ladies. I have to speak to everyone about their personal belongings, but your brother is a different issue. I'll have to talk to Mr. Maynard about you and your brother. Believe me, I know what a big responsibility you have on your hands. I had to take care of my own brother for years." Elly sighed, then asked the young lady, "Why do you want to leave your home here?"

"The bank has taken our farm, our home, and I had two days to pack up and get off our property. I tried working the land, but it ain't easy for a gal alone. I sold eggs and butter to keep food on the table, but I have no money to pay taxes or pay back the loan my pa borrowed from the bank. I ain't got no choice but to leave. And golly, Miss Eddy, I ain't got no place to go. I ain't even got a job. Well, that ain't true. There's Wild Bill's place and he's just waiting for me."

Elly stared at the defeated young girl's face. This girl had grit and would never give in to that saloon owner. "While I talk to Mr. Maynard, you'll have to go through your things and take only what is necessary. Some of your furniture will have to be left behind. We may be able to sell some of your items before we depart in three days. I can't promise anything, but I will speak up for you and your brother and encourage Mr. Maynard to let you both travel with us."

"Oh, I can't thank you enough, ma'am. I just gotta leave this area and get a new start."

"You do remember that this is a wagon train of mail-order brides? A young child might hurt your chances of getting a husband. Have you thought of that?"

"If those men don't like children, then they won't like me." Mattie took her brother's hand and strode over to their horse and wagon.

Elly watched the young girl and her brother unpack their life's belongings from the wagon. After she'd spoken with several of the other brides-to-be, Elly felt more confident. Yes, she could handle this big responsibility. Most of the girls understood they couldn't bring their furniture, trunks and personal items. Elly explained to them that the trip was long, and the oxen, mules and horses pulling their wagons couldn't carry heavy loads across rivers and the desert-like conditions of the land.

By lunch, Elly had spoken with all ten ladies going on the trip. Major would stop at two other towns on their way and pick up more brides he had signed on. Twenty-eight brides would make the long trip to Sunflower, Texas, to meet their prospective husbands.

"Major, sir, I need a word with you," called Elly as he prepared to climbed over the tailgate into his wagon.

"Can it wait? I usually take a short rest about this time every day, and I'm plain tuckered out."

"It's important that I speak with you now. I have to come to a decision about one of your brides-to-be."

"All right, spit it out and let's be done with it. I hate anything hanging over my head while I'm trying to rest."

"Mattie Mathews, a young pretty girl that signed up to go with you, has brought her five year-old brother with her."

"What? We aren't taking on children. The ladies understood that." Major leaned against the side of the wagon and rolled a cigarette.

"Please, Major. I spoke at length with this young woman. She has no choice but to bring her brother along on this trip. They have lost their parents, and farm, and they have no place to go. The bank gave them two days to get off the property. If we don't allow her to travel with us, then her only other choice is to work for Wild Bill.

Do you want her to have to do that?"

"Don't even try putting that monkey on my back, gal. You know my answer to that dumb question." He dropped his cigarette and stomped it out with his boot.

"I have instructed her to go through her furniture and things and set most of them aside. Maybe some of it can be sold in the next day or two."

"So, you have already given this young woman hope that I'll allow her to come with us with her brother in tow?"

"I gave her hope, that's all. I told her it was your decision to make, not mine."

"All right. She can come with us, but I am making you and you alone responsible for her and her little brother. This is a rough trip and that child will have to be watched at all times. His big sister has work to do on this trip just like all the others. Understood?"

"I do. I have already planned to ask Mrs. Duffy if she will help watch after him during the day. He can ride in our wagon and keep her company. She'll be like a grandmother to him." Elly smiled, then winced from the sunburn she'd gotten from sitting in the sun while interviewing the women.

"Women," muttered Major as he climbed into his wagon.

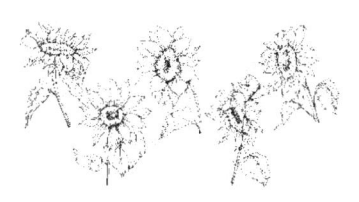

Chapter 8

"Good morning, ladies," Tate Maynard yelled to the group of brides. "We'll be staying here in Leesville for a few more days. This will give you time to take care of any personal business before we leave. You'll have a lot to learn to make this hard trip successful. My men and I'll try to prepare you for the rough trails that we'll be traveling on, the bad weather you'll have to endure and the wild animals and ground critters you'll have to watch out for. This is not a pleasure trip. We'll cross miles of flat plains, a few small mountains and a scorching desert before we reach Sunflower, Texas." Tate surveyed the ladies' faces and continued on with his speech.

"When you come back tomorrow, wear loose clothing, a man's hat and boots, or at least good sturdy shoes. You will ride your horse like a man—no sidesaddles." Some of the ladies sucked in their breath when he mentioned loose clothing, but he didn't care. They'd die out in this heat with corsets and layers of crinoline.

"If you have a parasol that would be helpful, too. We will supply all the tools that are needed on this trip, but if you have an extra hammer, some nails, a knife or any other useful tool you'll need, please bring them along." Tate watched the ladies for any reaction that might need to be addressed.

"When we're ready to form the wagon train, each wagon will

have a certain position in the line. You'll stay that way until one of my men directs you to the end of the line. Each wagon will take turns in the back of the train for a day at a time. I don't want to hear any squalling about the dust and the smells that you'll have to endure that day. No one will receive special treatment." The ladies' expressions remained impassive, and they didn't make any comments, so he addressed another problem.

"If you have any medicine or medical supplies at home, please bring them along, too. We don't have a doctor traveling with us, so whatever you bring might be helpful on this trip. Any questions?"

Major stood next to a wagon, listening to his son's talk to the brides, nodding when Tate didn't brook any arguments or excuses from any of them.

"This is going to be a long, rough trip, but my pa and I have made this journey many times, and I'm sure we'll have a successful trip if you all pull your own weight and pitch in and help." He paused and gave each woman a hard stare. "If you are not prepared to learn and work hard, you'd better pack up your gear and head back from where you came." Tate stopped talking and waited for the ladies to decide.

"All right," he said, as all the brides stood their ground. "I'm going to ask some questions, and if any of you know how to do some of the things I name, please step this way." He glanced around. "If you can handle a team of horses or mules, please step this way." He waved his hand to his right.

Two young women stepped forward. "Good, you will help my men teach some of the other ladies. Do any of you know how to ride a horse?" Most of the women moved toward him.

"Good, because we'll need outside riders to help guard the wagon train during the day. Can any of you shoot a handgun, shotgun, or rifle?"

"Great," Tate shouted as most of the women moved closer to him. "I want every one of you to know how to handle a gun and how to shoot it. I'm not expecting sharpshooters, but it's important you know how to protect yourself from man and beast."

Tate noticed Elly hadn't moved at all. She had some papers in her hand and was busy taking notes. He strolled over to her and lowered the papers from her face. "Miss Elly, can you do anything that I've asked the other ladies, like ride a horse, shoot, or drive a team?"

Tilting her chin a little higher, she answered his question. "I'm not going to be a bride, so I don't have to know how to do any of those things."

"Those things, as you put it, have nothing to do with being a bride. Those things are important for the ladies to know for survival on this trip. Now, if you can't ride, drive a team or shoot, you'll learn before we push on. Understand?" He shifted from one foot to the other as he waited for her answer. She would do as the others, or he might just leave her here in Leesville.

"And if I refuse?" Elly glared into his challenging eyes.

He stepped toward her, inches from her face. "You'll learn to do all these things, or you'll stay right here in Leesville. Got that?"

"Your father might have something to say whether I go or not, mister," Elly said, taking a step back and then poked her finger in his chest.

"You don't want to bring my pa into our discussion. He'll tell me to handle the problem, and I'm man enough to do just that. Now, get your fanny over there with the other ladies before I embarrass you."

She glanced at the other women, who pretended not to be watching who would win the disagreement these two headstrong people were having. They probably couldn't hear the words he said to her, but the expression on his face brooked no argument.

"I'll allow you to win this argument because I need to set an example for the other ladies, but no man will manhandle me without being sorry." Elly pasted a smile on her face and moseyed toward the group of ladies who needed help with some of the things Mr. Maynard said they must learn.

The ladies greeted her warmly to their group. "We'll all learn everything together," a young girl called Margaret, who looked about eighteen, said. She smiled at Elly as she re-plaited her pigtails. "Don't worry, Miss Elly, we'll help you."

A tall gal named Misty eased over to Elly. "Hey, Miss Elly, do you think we can get some pants like you're wearing at the dry goods store?"

The question surprised her. She had noticed the ladies giving her the once-over, but no one had said anything until now. "I guess so, but I'm wearing britches because I have only one dress. All my clothes burned in the town fire, but my brother's clothes were saved. I'm wearing his clothes, but the young Mr. Maynard doesn't approve of them," she said laughing.

"I love the way they fit, and you can move around out here with so much ease. If Mr. Maynard don't like them, we can wear them under our skirts." Misty smiled and the others nodded.

"All right, ladies," Tate called. "Now I know what some of you can or cannot do, and the men will begin working with you. Hank here will take you to your wagon so you can load your belongings in it. Remember the instructions Miss Eddy gave you about taking items that aren't necessary. There'll be two ladies to a wagon. You can choose your partner yourself, or if you like, Miss Eddy can assign someone for you."

Before the ladies dispersed, Tate said, "Remember, this will be your home for the next several months. Keep it clean. There will be no open food kept in your wagon. You don't want to attract bugs, snakes, or even bears coming around at night. Use common sense."

He circled around the group, and some of his men gathered close. "As soon as you've made your wagon comfortable, come back and join the men. They'll introduce you to your team of animals that you'll be responsible for. You are to care for them and the equipment to harness them."

Hank Johnson, an out rider, strolled over to the brides-to-be. "First off, you gotta get familiar with the animals, so when you start learning to drive the wagon, they'll listen to your commands." He leaned over and spat a stream of tobacco juice near the ladies' feet. "As you learn to harness and unharness your mules and horses, you'll check their equipment for weak areas that could break on the trail. At the end of the day, wash your horse's back and their legs from the knees down. This will help prevent sores. The men will help you tie them to a picket line each night."

Tate noticed that some of the ladies were not listening to Hank, but giving him side glances. He was a young bachelor who'd been called handsome many times. Several of the women wanted his personal attention, and Tate was tired of it. "My men are good teachers, so listen to them and do as they say. We want to pull out of Leesville by the end of the week. We'll only stop in one other town and pick up eight more brides. The fever has spread through Little Rock, so we'll bypass that town on this trip."

Tate glanced around at the ladies. "Again, I asked if any of you have questions."

"Yes sir, I have one. Do you care if some of us ladies wear men's trousers like Miss Eddy? I know I could ride and move around better without these long skirts." A young woman with reddish hair and a spray of golden freckles across her pretty face, Peg Driver was waiting for his reply.

Tate whirled around and glared at Elly. "Go ahead, but if and when we stop in a town, you'll dress like ladies."

The women began to whisper among themselves, and some even giggled at the possibility of dressing in more comfortable clothing as they followed the men for their lessons on survival.

Tate passed Elly, who was headed to the wagon with the other ladies, and he grunted to her under his breath. "See what you started."

Elly offered a jaunty grin and continued walking. That man could be irritating, she thought.

After what seemed like hours, Elly completed her first horseback-riding lesson. Her backside ached and the skin between her thighs had been rubbed raw. But all in all, she was proud of herself for being able to saddle the mount, even if she did have to stand on a large crate to toss it across the horse's back.

Once she rode back to the corral, a young cowboy named Slim met her and held the reins. He shoved a stepping box close to the horse for her to use to dismount. Elly limped away with the horse still following her. Slim caught up to her, reached for her gloved hand and removed the horse's reins. "I'll rub him down and feed him for you today since it's your first lesson and all."

Elly gladly accepted his offer. "Thank you," she whispered and limped toward her wagon.

***

Leaning against her wagon wheel, Tate tossed a piece of hay from his mouth and grinned at her. "I'll let you get away with not caring for your mount today, but from now on, you'll tend to your own horse. Slim was just being nice because he knows your pretty little behind took a good pounding on that saddle today." Tate sauntered toward the corral laughing at his own joke.

Early the next morning, the ladies lined up to continue their lessons for riding, saddling, driving the wagons, and caring for the animals. Since Elly needed to learn more about riding and saddling her horse, Slim was willing to give her more instructions.

"I know how to saddle the horse, but I need to ride more so my horse learns my commands. The poor animals goes right when I want him to go left and speeds up with I want him to slow down," she said, shaking her head.

"Ride around in the corral, and I'll help you. You'll learn to press your knees into his sides and gently pull on the reins," Slim said.

Tate joined Slim in the corral. He glanced at Elly. "You're a determined gal, aren't you? You need to do something else and let your backside and legs heal." When their gazes clashed, he tossed a cold stare in her direction.

Elly returned his glare of ice. "Like you said, I'm determined, and I'll ride again today."

"Don't come back whining to me or my men. They'll not be coddling you anymore."

Her eyes filled with a mist of tears behind her eyelids, but she looked away. He was right, but she didn't care. She clenched her fists and held them at her sides. What she wouldn't do to pound him into the ground for being so—right.

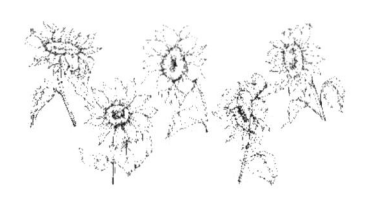

Chapter 9

Tate stepped away from Elly as she saddled the horse to ride. "Elly, I'm serious. You really need to find something else to do today. I remember what it was like learning to ride my first time." Tate said, knowing that her behind had to be sore from yesterday.

"Really? I'm surprised you can remember that far back."

"All right, smarty pants. When you can't walk or sit for a few days, don't come whining to me. But before we pull out, you'll still need to know how to shoot a gun."

"Go take care of some other business, and don't worry about what I learn or don't." Elly climbed on her horse and kicked him in the side harder than she should have. The horse lunged forward, causing Elly to scream.

The strange sound startled the animal. Spooked, the horse reared up on his back legs and jumped forward again. Elly jerked on the reins and screamed again, frightening the animal more. The animal took off at a full gallop across the corral and jumped the fence. Elly had leaned forward onto the horse's neck, grabbing its mane as they flew across the three-foot fence and out into the prairie.

Tate and Slim stood frozen as they watched the pair jump the fence and race away. Major had just ridden up to the corral when he witnessed Elly fly over the fence into the open field.

"Get down and give me your horse, Pa." Major leaped to the ground, and Tate jumped on the horse's back and chased after Elly.

Tate was riding as fast as his horse could go when he caught sight of Elly. The horse was racing along the edge of a deep ditch. "Please Lord," he prayed. "Don't let the horse ride down into that water."

In a flash of a second, Elly tumbled off the horse and rolled into the deep ditch filled with murky water.

"Elly!" Tate called over and over as he raced to the edge of the stinking ditch with weeds growing over four-feet tall along its border.

"Here I am. Help me," a scared kitten of a voice replied.

Tate jumped off the horse and stopped at the edge. Elly lay on her back, her arms stretched over her head and her face spattered with mud. If the situation weren't so bad, Tate would have laughed.

"Elly, are you all right? Are you hurt anywhere?"

"No, I don't think I'm hurt, but be careful. I slid down into a hole and I'm stuck. My boots are filled with water and mud, and I can't move my feet. Please pull me out of this nasty water. I'm freezing to death."

"If you hadn't been so hardheaded, you wouldn't be in this ditch. I told you to stay off that horse today," Tate scolded without thinking about how scared she must be.

"Do you always have to be right? Just shut up and help me," she cried.

He shouldn't have scolded her. She could possibly be hurt. Tate stepped back to the ditch's edge, removed his cowboy boots and rolled his pants up as high as he could.

"I'm coming into the water to get you. Don't try to move until I reach you." Tate stepped down into the muddy water and prayed he didn't step on something slimy. "I'm here now, sweetheart. Are you hurt anywhere?"

"I don't think so. Just scared of what might be in this muddy water."

I'm going to pull you up. Try to wiggle your feet out of your boots." Tate placed his hands under her armpits. His hands brushed the sides of her breasts, and he could hear her draw in a breath.

"I've got you." Every muscle strained as he pulled her out of her boots. She leaned back against him, causing him to lose his balance and flop back in the water. "Whoa," Tate yelled as his back hit the cold water. "Damnit," he stormed, "What a mess." He managed to stand with mud plastered to seat of his pants.

"I'm free," Elly yelled, "but my boots are still stuck in the mud. Help me. I've got to get them," she yelled and stooped down into the thick water and bumped him from the rear. Tate fell back again into the dark water, splaying mud onto his face and neck. "Come on, woman. Let's get out of this swamp before something bites us."

Elly felt around in the mud until she found one of the boots. "Got one," she said, then squatted, holding her chin above the water, until she discovered the other one. Elly tried with all her might to pull the shoe up to the top of the water, but the suction of the mud made it impossible for her to get it.

"Help me, Tate. I need my shoes," she explained. "They're brand new."

"Come on, woman. Get up so I can pull you out of the water. To hell with the shoes," he yelled.

Disgusted by the mud covering him, he grabbed Elly and flopped her into the tall grass at the edge of the ditch. He began climbing up the slope when Elly pushed him back down.

"No, I can't leave my other boot. Mrs. Duffy just bought them for me, and I have to have them," Elly said, her lip quivering.

"Oh hell," Tate snorted, "Sit still and I'll get it. Just what I need is a squalling woman," he said. In a single movement, he pulled up the other boot. After showing it to her, he turned it upside down and emptied the mud, then tossed the wet boot on the bank and rinsed his hands. He started to dry his hands on his pants, but they were caked with thick mud from his waist down. "What a damn mess," he sputtered.

Chapter 10

Shivers ran up her spine when he lifted her to the bank of the ditch. Although both of them were slick with mud, he flopped down on the bank, pulled her across his hard thighs and settled her onto his lap. Elly had no idea why she felt secure. Why his light touch made her trust him instead of feeling afraid. She shivered as she felt herself leaning against his solid chest. "Thanks for getting my boot," Elly said with a shaky voice. "I'm sorry to be a burden. I'm useless when it comes to riding."

"Quiet," he spoke for the first time. He pulled her closer to his chest. His hands were rough and cold as he held her. She'd have more bruises on her skin later.

They sat quietly gazing into each other's eyes. His mouth came down hard on hers, kissing her with force. She sat frozen, wanting to respond to his passion but didn't dare. The kiss ended, but oh, what a wonderful memory she would have.

When he lowered his face to kiss her again, she finally spoke. "Please Tate, don't." Though her heart was pounding, she mustn't allow this man to try and take control of her body. Her thoughts were already occupied with his every movement, every minute since she met him.

She peered up at him, and his mouth softened. The pride in his eyes told her he would not harm her in any way—a way that she wasn't ready for.

He took her hands and pulled her up on her bare feet. With a firm grip, he led her to his horse. "Do you think you can ride? Are you hurt anywhere that you aren't telling me?" He practically pulled her to where his horse stood.

"I'm afraid to get back on a horse. I don't ever want to ride again," she whined while trying to free the grip he had on her hand.

"You'll sit in front of me on the way back to the wagons. Later, I'll get you a better mount that is well-trained."

"Please don't bother. I'll walk beside the wagons or ride in the chuck wagon with Henry. I'm too afraid, and you aren't going to make me either." Elly tilted her chin up toward him, her face only inches from his.

Tate gazed down and felt himself drowning in her eyes. Her complexion, even sprinkled with black mud, was as clear as a spring sky. Her ebony eyelashes contrasted with the brilliant green of her eyes. He had been near this smart-mouthed girl many times, but he'd never noticed how beautiful she was. "We'll talk about this later," he said and used his handkerchief to wipe some of the wet mud off her face.

"You heard me, Mr. Boss Man. No more horses for me."

Tate's strong arms lifted her in the air and placed her on the saddle. His hands removed some mud from his pants and climbed behind her before she knew what was taking place. "Sit still and lean back against me. I know I smell about as good as you, but that can't be helped. Rest. I'm sure you're worn out and hurting. We'll be back at the wagons soon. The horse carried you nearly two miles across the prairie before he stopped."

Elly sat astride the saddle in front of Tate and held on for dear life. When the horse moved, her body tensed and she wanted to scream, but she bit down on her bottom lip. The wet clothes were cold, and the wind made it worse.

"Relax, Elly," Tate whispered in her ear. His hot breath smelled of mint and his day's growth of whiskers rubbed against the back of her neck. His shirt sleeves smelled of sweat, mixed with the scent of horse flesh and dirty water, but she tried to make herself relax. She focused on the sky before closing her eyes.

Tate rode his big bay into the circle of wagons. The ladies stood around bonfires, warming their hands. Everyone was too worried about Elly to do their chores, even though Major ordered them to get busy.

Major hurried over to Tate, lifted Elly down into his arms and carried her like a baby to her wagon. Mrs. Duffy stood outside waiting to lower the tailgate.

Tate tied the two horses to the side of Elly's wagon and waited for his pa to return. "Thank the good Lord she doesn't have any broken bones," Major commented as he threw his long leg over the tailgate. "Where did you find her? She stinks to high heaven and so do you."

"I'll meet you over at the fire and we can talk. I want to give Mrs. Duffy some water to help wash Elly," he said and grabbed two buckets off the side of their wagon, then filled them with water from the attached barrels.

The major untied the two horses and walked a few paces before giving the reins to one of the men. "Be sure to rub them both down good and give them an extra helping of oats."

As Tate carried the water to Mrs. Duffy's, he heard his pa say, "Miss Eddy is all right. She's bruised and battered, and muddy from her head to her toes, but she isn't hurt badly. I'm sure after a bath and rest, she'll be just fine.

The sun peeked through the opening of the brown, corded curtain at the end of the wagon. Elly moaned and pulled the quilt over her head. Every muscle in her body hurt. If she was a child, she would plead with her mama to let her stay in bed.

"Morning, Elly," Mrs. Duffy said, patting Elly's leg.

"Morning to you, too, but I'm glad you didn't say good morning cause it's certainly not one." Elly groaned. Her backside and thighs ached with every movement. Slowly, she rose to her feet and got dressed. Today, she had to prepare the wagon for travel.

A minute after she climbed down from the wagon, Tate joined her. She was having a hard time pulling the ladder off the side of the wagon so Mrs. Duffy could climb down. With a single move, he reached over her head and set the ladder next to the wagon.

They stared at each other. The eyes that locked with hers were full of concern. For her? What was going on in that head of his? He was a gentle giant one minute, like when he had found her, and next a grumpy old bear, but now they were in a different place. He moved closer to her and whispered, "Are you well?"

"I'm all right, just sore from riding and taking that fall." She stepped away from his tall form.

"It's no wonder. That horse rode a couple of miles with you before he stopped. Do you remember if you fell off the horse while it was running or after he stopped?" His eyes flicked over her body.

"I'm not sure what happened. I must have hit my head because I have a large bump right here." Elly pointed to a spot beside her left ear. "I remember feeling a little dazed in the muddy water. When I tried to move, my boots were stuck and I knew that if I stood, I might be sucked down deeper. I was never so happy to see anyone when you showed up. Thank you for coming after me."

"I'm glad you aren't hurt any worse than you are." He whispered and gently coaxed her close to his chest.

Elly jerked her shoulders from his hands and whirled away from him. "What do you think you're doing?"

"What do you mean? After last night. . . . I thought . . . well, damnit woman, you let me kiss you. I just figured . . . well, I hoped we had an understanding."

"An understanding? You must be an egotistical fool. You saved my life and took care of me. I probably would have let the devil himself kiss me. Besides, we hardly know each other."

"I know you pretty darn well, Missy. You're a hardheaded gal who don't have the sense the good Lord gave a billy goat." Tate said, every vein in his neck pulsing. "If you had stayed off that blasted horse for another day or until your sassy behind got better, you probably could have handled your horse."

Giggling came from the back of the wagon from several of the women, who were watching and listening to their argument. "Now look what you've done," Elly whispered and stepped back from his tall frame.

"Look here, Miss-High-and-Mighty. You're the one screeching like a wild Comanche. If you learned to control your temper, we wouldn't have an audience every time we're together."

"I don't care," she hissed. "I'm fine. Thank you, now go away, so I can help Mrs. Duffy prepare our wagon for travel."

"I'm going." He pivoted and walked a few steps, then stopped. He sighed. His broad shoulders slumped and all traces of temper in his voice vanished. He gave Elly a hard stare and said, "Slim will help you lift the heavy things into your wagon."

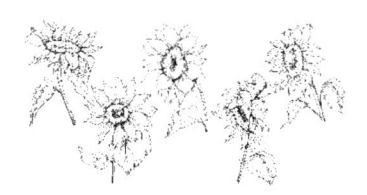

Chapter 11

After Elly and Mrs. Duffy enjoyed a nice breakfast and helped Henry clean up, they arranged their personal belongings in the wagon, their temporary home.

Tate laughed at Elly's attempt to drive the team of horses in with the others to form a train. The horses tossed their heads and nickered because of the way Elly was cutting their mouths with their bits. The team refused to walk in a straight line until Slim pulled his horse to the side of Elly's wagon and jumped up on the seat next to her.

"Let me give you a quick lesson on how to handle the old boys," Slim said. He clicked his tongue and whistled as the team set off in a straight line. "They'll follow the wagon ahead, but you must be gentle with the reins. One of the men will help you and Mrs. Duffy drive until you get the hang of it."

"I'll be happy to drive the wagon, if you teach me, Mr. Slim. I'm a big boy, and I can do a man's job," Johnny, the five-year-old son of Mattie Mathews, said as he peeked out from the wagon.

"That's mighty fine, son, but I think you need to get a little more meat on those bones of yours before you can control these big boys pulling this wagon. You sit back and take care of Mrs. Duffy. She'll probably read to you and let you color some pretty pictures while we're traveling."

"Mrs. Duffy is getting some paper and pencils for Johnny now so he can stay busy while his mama is driving their wagon," Elly said.

"Sure nice of you to allow the young woman to bring her boy. We've made this trip many times, but Major never let a kid travel with us."

"I had no idea. It's a wonder Tate let him tag along."

"Tate's a good man. Treats his men real well, and the pay's good, too," Slim said as he peered around.

"What you looking for?"

"Just making sure everyone is in line and none of the wagons are lagging behind. That's my job, to keep the wagons straight and close together." He handed back the reins and settled on the bench. Just as he was starting to relax, Elly tugged on the reins.

"Watch out," Slim called. "You're pulling too hard. Ease off on the reins. You don't want to cause one of the horses to rear up, and then the rest of the team will act up. Just hold them like this," he said and placed both of his long arms around her shoulders and took her hands in his. "Feel how soft I'm holding the reins. Now you take them." He moved away from Elly.

As they neared the foothills, the undergrowth thickened, but the old worn trail was smooth in many places. Wildflowers grew close to the trail. Elly wished she was walking so she could pick a bouquet. The wagon trail continued until it widened again. Off in the distance, a sea of bluebonnets were in bloom. Elly admired the flowers for as long as she could see them.

Tate rode past the wagons and signaled for everyone to stop. It was time for the noon meal. Elly pulled on the brake and her team stopped. "That was very good," Slim responded. "I believe you have the hang of it, but if you feel nervous, just holler."

"Thanks, Slim," she said, then climbed onto the big front wheel and leaped to the ground. Every part of her body hurt from hitting the ground. "I'd better go and help Henry get lunch. Later, some of the ladies will ride with him and peel potatoes and other vegetables for the dinner meal."

"After we eat, Henry will take the chuck wagon with a few of the women. They'll go ahead of us and set up camp for the night," Slim said. "One wagon can travel a lot faster than a train of wagons."

"I had forgotten about that. Makes sense since Henry has to cook for so many people." Elly stretched her back and limped over to the chuck wagon. Thank goodness she didn't have to carry buckets of water to the horses.

Tate had ridden ahead to check out the river crossing. He sat on his horse and watched the flow of the river. From where he sat, he could see a good distant down the riverbank. The water was much higher along the bank than it was the last time he traveled this way. The hot sun shone down on him. What he wouldn't do to jump in the river and take a good bath, but he thought better of it. A couple of his men joined him, with one of them surveying the situation. "What do you think, Tate," asked Jerome, a young cowboy who had just started shaving.

"The water's much deeper than before. Let's ride further down the bank. We might find an easier crossing."

After lunch Tate arrived back at the wagon train and explained to the women that the river was higher than before because of the summer rains, but the men had found a safe place to cross. "We have crossed this river many times, and we've yet to lose anyone. Drivers of the wagons will have to hold tight to the reins of their teams. Some of the men will ride beside each wagon and help lead your horses across. Any questions?" Tate looked around at the concerned expressions on the ladies' faces.

As the group began moving to their assigned wagons, he noticed Elly shaking her head from side to side. "What wrong now, Missy?" Somehow Tate knew Elly was going to give him a problem, but he didn't know why.

"I'm not driving that wagon into the water, and you can't make me. Get one of the men to drive it across," Elly demanded, her hands posted on her hips and her eyes defiant.

His neck heated up, the way it did when someone crossed him. "I'm not giving you a choice. You made your decision when you signed up to travel on this wagon train. By your actions, you gave yourself into my care. You will drive your wagon across the river, or you'll ride horseback. I don't have enough men to give you special treatment. All the other ladies will pull their weight and you will, too."

Elly's eyes opened wide, then she covered her mouth, spun around, and ran behind a wagon.

Tate followed fast on her heels in time to hear her emptying her stomach into a pail in the wagon. Mrs. Duffy was speaking softly to her as she patted her back. When the retching stopped, Mrs. Duffy encouraged her to lie down.

"Mrs. Duffy," Tate called to the older woman, "hand me the pail and I'll empty and wash it for you."

"Oh, Tate," Mrs. Duffy said, as she glanced down at him. "The child is sick, but I have her lying down now. A clean bucket of water would be nice."

"Please, Elly, take a sip of water and rinse your mouth out. You'll feel better," Mrs. Duffy begged. Elly leaned forward, rinsed her mouth and spit into the clean pail, then she took another drink.

The next morning was spent preparing the inside of the wagons. The ladies stacked everything from the floor as high as they could to keep it dry.

While the men and women prepared to eat lunch, Elly's stomach had been queasy since yesterday, but she served Tate a plate of beans, ham, boiled potatoes and biscuits. He held out his tin mug for some coffee, not aware that he was her enemy.

Once everyone had lunch, she refused to continue to think about what lay ahead this afternoon. She'd concentrate on the lovely, rich land that surrounded the river instead of the danger. "Oh, Lord, please help me have courage to drive my wagon across the swift water," she mumbled to herself as she walked on the sandy bank.

Johnny ran up to her and took her hand. "Can I walk with you? Mrs. Duffy said I couldn't walk close to the river without a grown-up. You're a grown-up, ain't you, even though I hear her call you 'child' sometimes?"

Laughing for the first time in days, Elly replied, "Yes, you may walk with me. Maybe we can find some wild berry bushes or flowers to pick." Elly reached down and took the little boy's small hand in her.

"The river looks pretty, don't it? I sure wish I could take off my clothes and go for a swim. Do you know how to swim, Miss Elly?"

"No, I never learned, but you're so young. How do you know how to swim?"

"We had a pond near our farm, and one day my pa and me walked into the water, and the next thing I knew, I went flying through the air and made a big splash. I went down and down into the water and when I popped up, I heard Pa screaming for me to swim or drown. I went down, and again I came up at the bank. I fooled him. I swimmed like a fish under the water." He grinned up at Elly.

"Mercy, I wouldn't want to learn like that," Elly said thinking how scary that would be. "The water isn't safe to swim in today. Maybe we will come to another river that isn't as swift as this one. The rain last night has made this water very deep."

Elly and Johnny didn't hear Tate ride up behind them until he spoke. "You don't strike me like the kind of woman who wouldn't be willing to learn to swim. You rode a horse, even though you were afraid, and you learned to drive a big team of mules. Why would you be afraid to get into some water and swim?" Tate dropped his leg over the saddle horn

"I never said I was afraid to learn to swim. What are you doing eavesdropping on our conversation?" Elly lifted her chin high toward the handsome ramrod.

"I asked you a question. Why haven't you learned to swim?"

"If you must know, Mr. Nosy Body, I have always been too busy to spend hours away from my home or my job. I've worked hard all my life to take care of myself. I never had the time for swimming or horseback riding or all the other things people do for pleasure. Now go away and let Johnny and me have a few minutes of leisure time."

"I'll go for now, but turn around and head back to the wagons. We'll be pulling out in an hour." Tate touched his hat and gave her a little salute as he rode away.

Elly watched the big man ride away. She kicked a rock into the tall grass. A big snake head appeared and it moved a few paces. Johnny screamed at the sight. Elly grabbed him around the waist and began running back up the sandy bank toward the wagons.

"Run, Miss Elly," Johnny yelled again.

Breathing hard and fast, Elly stopped and placed the youngster down and started laughing. "We're safe now," she said after reaching the wagons. "I guess I woke that snake up from his nap. We scared him, and he sure scared us."

"Hey, mama," Johnny yelled. "Miss Elly threw a rock at a giant snake and it came after us. We ran fast and got away from it."

As Elly stooped down to Johnny's level, she saw Tate sitting on his horse listening to Johnny spew his wild tale about the snake adventure. "Now, Johnny, that wasn't what happened at all. I didn't intentionally wake the snake, and he didn't come after us."

Tate peered down at Elly and shook his head as he rode away.

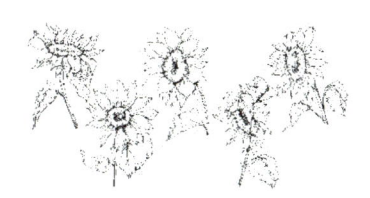

Chapter 12

At the end of the day, all the wagons had crossed the river safely without losing anyone or any of the livestock. Tate was proud of all the women, especially Elly, although he would never mention it. At one point, he was afraid that one of the men was going to have to jump in her wagon and take the reins, but the lead horse finally settled down and she was able to make a good crossing.

Once all the wagons and the animals were safe in their circle, corralled and fed for the night, the evening meal was ready, already prepared by Henry and a few of the ladies who had gone ahead. Most of the ladies had been nervous about driving their wagons across the swift water. Settling into the night without having to gather wood or cook was a treat.

Tate sat on a log drinking a cup of hot coffee when two ladies walked by, pointing at the younger men and giving Tate a sweet smile. The giggling girls hurried past and disappeared into the dark. He wasn't going to put up with flirting on his watch, so he was going to have to speak to Elly about this situation. These brides were traveling to Sunflower to meet their prospective grooms who had already paid passage for them. He had never delivered a bunch of soiled doves, and he wasn't about to start with this trip.

Over the years he had earned a reputation for bringing decent women to towns to become brides. He'd hired good men, but having to stay away from women for weeks on end could cause them to break the rules of the wagon train. The way some of the younger women were strutting around could cause a saint to be lead astray.

Elly appeared and motioned him to scoot over and allow her to sit. She looked like she had something to say. He quickly stood and waited for her to sit down before he got comfortable on the log again.

"I want to speak with you about a problem I need you to address," she said.

"What a coincidence. I was just coming to find you."

"Oh? What do you need to talk with me about?" she asked, her eyes wide.

"Ladies first. What problem do you need me to solve for you?"

"Well, I wanted to speak to you about your men. They seem to be too friendly with some of the brides-to-be. You need to keep your men away from the ladies, especially at night." Elly looked off into the dark.

"My men? Ha, that's too funny. It's part of your job to control the ladies and their 'encouraging.' I just witnessed two young girls walking by here batting their eyes and shaking their behinds at my younger men and . . . me. I was going to tell you to reign in their claws. If anything is going on, it's because the girls are provoking my men. You'd better tell them to behave themselves or I will put them off this wagon train at the next town. And if you can't do your job, you can be replaced too."

"Well, I never. It seems we both have a problem. You tell your men to behave themselves and I'll instruct my brides again about their conduct." Elly stormed away.

"Well, boss man," laughed Slim. "I guess you set her straight."

"Quiet. And you'd better watch your step around some of the girls. I have eyes. I see them watching you ride past and how they serve you larger portions of the grub."

"Me?" he said, his hands on his chest. "I can't help it if they're crazy about me—the handsome fellow that I am."

"Well, Romeo, you'd better watch your step around some of those silly gals or you'll be out of a job. I'm serious this time, Slim. Some of the 'ladies' are different from the ones we've transported before. This is going to be my last trip, and I don't want to end it with a bad name for bringing the wrong kind of women to my paying customers."

"Hey, man. I didn't know you were planning on quitting the bride business. Are you and your pa going to settle down on your land in Sunflower? I sure would like to work for you on your ranch, if that would be a possibility?"

"Be proud to have you work for us, but don't mention this to anyone, please. We'll have a lot to do to get settled on the ranch."

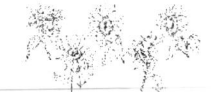

Without much discussion with his father, Tate had the ladies circle the wagons and prepare for a mid-morning stop. They'd reached the outskirts of Orange Grove, Texas, where four young brides-to-be were waiting.

"Elly, have the ladies who would like to go into town be prepared to leave in about thirty minutes. Jeremy will drive the wagon to the general store. They are not to go anywhere else in town. Slim will pick up the new brides and return to the wagon train where we can get them settled in. We'll be staying here the rest of the day and depart early in the morning as usual. The girls are not to wear those men's trousers into town." Tate yelled the instruction loud enough for all the ladies to hear.

Tate's horse slogged through muddy water on their way to the general store in town. Orange Grove was a small town with only a general store, a café, a small church at the end of the street, and a building that held the post office and telegraph. A livery was at the other end of the street with a red barn built behind it.

When he reached the general store, two young ladies smiled at him from a bench near the double doors. "Howdy, ladies," Tate said as he removed his Stetson. "Are you ladies waiting for the wagon train to Sunflower?"

"Yes, sir," a tall blonde who looked to be in her late twenties replied. "There's two more girls in the store who plan to go with us. Are you the leader of the wagon train?"

"Yes, my name is Tate Maynard and my pa is called Major. I have a wagon coming into town to take you and the other ladies out to the wagon train and help get you settled. Can any of you ladies drive a team of mules or horses?"

"We can because we were raised on farms all our lives," the blond girl commented.

"Good. My man, Slim, will be here in a few minutes. Sit tight," Tate said before entering the store.

"Howdy," a toothless clerk behind the counter said. "What can I do for you today?" He leaned around Tate to get a better look at the front porch. Tate glanced over his shoulder in time to see what the old man was trying to see.

"Is there something wrong, old man?"

"Well, ain't none of my business, but I don't want no trouble in my store."

"What kind of trouble are you expecting? If it's anything to do with me, I'd like to know about it."

"Well, it's like this. Those two, twin sisters by the rack—," he nodded at the two girls in the store, "they're young and wild-acting most of the time. Their pa ain't going to take to them running off to get married. He's probably on his way into town about now, and if not, he'll set upon your wagon train in two shakes," he whispered while watching the girls hiding behind a rack of dresses.

"Is that the two girls over in the corner of the store? The two redheads?" Tate said looking in their direction.

"Yep, that's them."

Tate strode to the racks and stopped in front of the pretty twin girls. "Ladies, my name is Mr. Maynard. Are you planning to go on my wagon train to Sunflower to get married?"

Both of their heads bobbed up and down.

"Do you have permission from your folks to go with me?" When neither responded, Tate said, "It's like this. You can't travel with me without permission because you appear young. Are you eighteen yet?"

"We were told you only had to be sixteen and we're sixteen, so we're old enough. Pa don't care if we go." One of the twins mumbled the last part.

"I'm sorry, girls. You are both very pretty, and I know some young men would love to have you for their brides, but without your folk's permission, I can't take you."

"You can't or won't?" the other twin spoke for the first time, her tone sharp. Tate gave her a look that spoke volumes about her attitude.

He turned on his heels. "I'm not taking you, so you'd better hurry back home before your folks miss you," Tate said over his shoulder. Tate glanced back at the twins. They were whispering to each other, most likely planning another scheme that would land them into trouble.

As Tate prepared to tell the clerk what he needed, a giant of a man burst through the door causing Tate and the clerk to jump. "Where are they?"

"We're here, Pa," the twins answered at the same time. "We come here to get some thread, and we're ready to go home now."

"Well, all right then," he said in a softer voice. "Your ma is in the wagon waiting on you."

Watching the two girls sashay across the room and wave goodbye, the big man marched over to the counter. "They don't have me fooled for one minute. I don't know what changed their minds, but I'm shore glad. I didn't want to bust anyone up, but I was prepared to do it."

"Well, Judd, it's because this here fellow refused to take them. Told them to go home cause they were too young. That's what he said, and they didn't like it one bit." The old storekeeper looked proud to tell the story.

"Is that right, Mister?" Judd asked.

"Yes, sir. They didn't have your permission, and I don't take child brides on my train. Most of my men want mature women who are willing to bear children and work hard on their farms right beside them. Your girls will grow up one day and make some men very happy," Tate said.

"Well, thanks again for not taking them." The big man strode out of the store and got into the wagon beside his wife. Tate watched the young girls swing their legs from the tailgate and laugh. So young, he thought.

Tate returned to the counter and grinned at the little man. "Thanks for the heads-up with those girls and their pa. I wouldn't have taken them, but it was good to know how their folks felt about it. I wouldn't want to tangle with that bear of a man," Tate said, laughing.

Slim entered the store and asked about the other brides. "There are only two ladies on the porch. Where are the others?"

"That's all the brides going from here. Oh, did Henry come with you or send a list?"

"He's coming in, but he stopped to look at the brooms on the front porch. Don't have any idea why he wants a broom." Slim walked over to the jar of peppermint candy and got himself a stick. He laid a penny on the counter.

"You get two sticks for a penny, mister," said the clerk. Slim reached into the jar and placed one in his shirt pocket for Johnny.

A lot of giggling and laughter came through the door and the clerk's eyes brightened. Rushing over to the women, he asked, "How can I help you ladies?" Tate laughed at the old man and busied himself choosing several sticks of candy.

Leaving the store, Tate noticed the two new brides-to-be were loaded in the wagon with their carpetbags thrown into the back. "Ladies, I must ask if you have permission from your folks to leave town and travel on my wagon train to Sunflower."

Both of the girls glanced at each other and gave him a sweet smile. "Mr. Maynard, I've been a widow for four years," said Mary Lou Thompson, a straight-nosed woman with hair twisted so tight it gave her a wild-eyed look.

Tate glanced at the other girl sitting tall and straight. "What's your story, young lady?"

"My folks have passed and I live with my brother and his wife. My sister-in-law is happy to see me go. You know the old saying, 'two women can't live under the same roof'? Well, that's true. Besides, I'm plenty old enough to make my own decisions."

Tate studied the dark-haired girl who was as cute as a kitten. "Well then, I am to understand I won't have to worry about an angry man coming after you."

Jeremy was at the old livery giving his two horses water. Tate called out. "Let's give the ladies about thirty minutes to make their purchases. Come with me for some coffee and a piece of pie while we wait on them."

Slim drove the two new brides to their wagon and helped them to get settled. He carried their bags and introduced them to the team of horses that would be pulling their wagon. Both ladies knew their way around horses and could drive a wagon—that thrilled him to death.

He directed the ladies to Elly's wagon where she introduced Mrs. Duffy to them. After Elly took down all the information about the girls, she told them once Henry arrived back from town, she would take them to the chuck wagon.

After supper everyone settled down from their exciting day of shopping in town. The new brides were made to feel welcome. Tate made an announcement. "Ladies, we are only about five days out from Sunflower, Texas. If the weather holds and we don't have any other unexpected delays, we should arrive on time."

Cheers were heard, and some of the ladies jumped up and danced around. Everyone was excited to learn their long journey would soon end and the beginning of their new futures would begin.

Elly had a lot to think about. Would she be able to teach school? She'd hoped to do something else. She wasn't going to be anyone's washwoman again, if she could help it. Maybe she could work in a café or bakery. She'd helped her mama make pies and bread to sell to the café and bakery in Leesville.

With the anticipation of arriving in a new place, she was too excited to go to bed, so she decided to walk around the wide circle of the wagons and back again. The night was lovely with bright stars in the dark sky. When Elly reached Mattie and Johnny's wagon, he practically fell out the back while asking her to take him to go pee. "Mattie's taking a bath and she ain't got no clothes on, and I've really got to go."

Elly could hear Mattie telling Johnny that he had to wait. "It's all right, Mattie, I'll take him with me. You enjoy your bath, and I'll bring him back in a little while."

Elly lifted the small boy down and took his hand. "Let's wait until we get away from the wagons where it's dark." Elly said as he pulled on her to hurry.

Elly and Johnny walked to the end of the wagons. "Go and do your business and I'll stand here with my back turned." Once he finished, he didn't walk back to Elly. In fact, she couldn't see him because of the darkness, but she could hear him.

"Ain't you the cutest little puppy I ever seen," Johnny said, "Where did you come from?"

"Johnny, where are you? Johnny, come to me this instant." Elly said, upset that he'd gotten away from her.

"Look, Miss Elly. Ain't he cute?" He carried the puppy into the light. "He came running to me. I patted him and he started licking me. I ain't never had a puppy. Can I keep him?"

Elly reached down and took the puppy out of Johnny's arms. "He's so healthy. The owner must be close by. We can't keep someone else's dog."

As Tate made his rounds, he noticed how unsettled the animals were in the corral area. Slim was talking to one of the horses and rubbing his nose to settle him down. "What's got the horses all stirred up tonight, Slim?"

"Not sure, Boss. They must smell a strange scent in the air. They're agitated for sure. The men standing guard haven't said anything, but I'll wager there's something nearby."

"Well, I'm walking around the circle. I'll keep a sharp eye," he said as he strolled toward the edge of the darkness.

"Elly." A voice she recognized came over her shoulder. "Put the pup down on the ground and back away. Take Johnny's hand and move slowly."

"Why? What's wrong with the puppy?" she asked but didn't move.

"Do as I said. *Now*," he said through gritted teeth. "That pup is a small wolf, and his mama is watching you right this minute. Her eyes and possibly the eyes of a pack of wolves are glowing in the darkness."

Elly lowered the pup to the ground while Johnny begged for her to give him the puppy. "Hush, Johnny," Tate said. "Elly, move behind me and keep walking to the wagons. I don't want to have to shoot the mama, but I will."

Elly took giant steps and hurried ahead of Tate. The puppy ran back toward its mama, and both of them disappeared into the night. Tate stood watching to make sure the pack of wolves were gone.

Johnny whimpered that he wanted that puppy. Tate picked the boy up and walked him to his wagon. "Listen, son," Tate said. "That pup was not a dog. He was a baby wolf. He will grow up and become a dangerous animal. Once you get settled in Sunflower with your sister, she will probably get you a dog. Many farms have several guard dogs."

Mattie reached out and took Johnny into her arms and thanked Tate for watching over him. "I'm sorry if he was any trouble."

Elly assured Mattie he was fine and that Tate found them in plenty of time. As she walked back to her wagon, Tate fell into step with her.

"I guess I did something stupid again. Go ahead and lay into me. I deserve it. I don't even know a dog from a wolf," she said and began to shake and tried to quell the brimming tears.

"I am thankful that I was walking the circle myself. The horses and mules were acting up. They must have picked up the wolves' scent. I kept looking into the darkness and I saw the glow of their eyes. That was a scary scene. It's hard to tell how many wolves are out there. They usually run in a pack."

"I should have watched Johnny more closely. I turned my back to give him some privacy and the next moment he was gone." Elly said. "I should have known better."

He stopped at the back of her wagon. "Listen, Elly, dog pups and little wolves look alike. It was natural for you to assume that the animal was a dog. Both of you are safe and that's what matters. I'm not angry with you, but I was afraid for just a minute. I thought the mama wolf might attack, but she was watching her baby."

"Thanks for saving Johnny and . . . me, again," Elly said before entering the back of her wagon.

Chapter 13

"They're here, the women are here!" a rider rode down the middle of Main Street of Sunflower screaming at the top of his lungs. "I saw them at Miller's pond." He jumped off his sweaty quarter horse, allowing the reins to hang loose as he strode through the bat-winged doors of the Golden Nugget Saloon.

One man spilled his beer all over himself when he heard the news. "You sure it's them?" Big Sal, the owner of the saloon, yelled back at the excited rider.

"Shore am. Give me a beer. My mouth's dryer than camel snot." Sal nodded at the bartender.

"Drink up and tell us what you seen at Miller's Pond. We're about to bust our britches while waiting for those gals to get here," a big cowboy shouted from a table with three other men playing a hand of cards.

"There be a whole pond of them—some young'uns and some a mite older. I saw one pretty blonde and one tall redhead. Most of them was getting ready to get in the water when one of the outriders seen me. He shot at me, but I think it was just a warning shot. I got the message and took off toward town as fast as I could to tell you gents to all get ready."

Tate rode into town looking for the sheriff. "His office is down thataway next to the dry goods store," said an old man sitting on the boardwalk whittling a stick. As Tate walked his horse toward the sheriff's office, he noticed a big white house with a rickety sign hanging loose that read, "Cozy Boardinghouse." The building appeared to be empty and sadly neglected.

When he arrived at the sheriff's office, a few fellows hurried across the dirt-packed street in his direction.

"Hey, Mister, are you in charge of the wagon train that has settled at Miller's Pond? The one with our brides?"

Tate laughed at their excited faces. "Yep, that's my train and it is carrying many brides-to-be. I came to talk to the sheriff about the men who ordered brides. Let me do business with him, and we'll make an announcement when I come back out." He jumped on the porch and went in.

"Good afternoon, Sheriff Murray, is it? I'm Tate Maynard. I have the brides that the Sunflower men ordered. I believe you sent the request for the ladies to my pa," Tate said and shook the older man's hand.

"Well, well, well. You arrived a few days ahead of schedule, but I don't think the men will care one bit. I have a list of the men who ordered brides—"

Tate interrupted him. "And I have the list of women who will be matched up with each man."

The sheriff wore black suspenders under a corded vest with a tin star pinned to it. He had a wide grin on his sunburned face. "We'll need to plan a get-together for the couples. I believe my Mildred and a few of her friends can start preparations today and have everything lined up by tomorrow morning. The whole town has been waiting on the ladies to arrive. We can hold the social in Mr. Gordon's barn because there's plenty of room to dance. What you say about the weddings taking place tomorrow evening?"

"Now, sheriff, I have one rule, and the men signed off on it when they paid their money. If any of my brides are not happy with the men we have chosen for them, or if any of the men aren't happy, they don't have to marry. I'll give them their money back. This is my last trip. My pa and I are going to settle down on our ranch here in Sunflower and raise cattle. Since this will be our home, I don't want a bunch of unhappy people living nearby," Tate said with a chuckle.

"Sounds good to me. I'll call in the men from their farms and ranches, and the ladies will get busy. We have a few men who will play music, so the couples can dance and get to know each other. The parson will be here and he can marry the ones who wish to begin their lives together."

Tate and the sheriff went outside and made a formal announcement to the men who had gathered outside the office. "Tomorrow evening, we will have a party to introduce the men and women who have signed up to become bride and groom. Now men, I expect you to come to this union sober, freshly bathed and in clean clothes. You want to make a good impression on your new bride-to-be. All of my ladies are to be treated with respect, and you are to act like the gentlemen your mamas taught you to be." All the men chuckled. "I'm sure you'll be happy with the young ladies I've brought for you to meet."

Tate stepped off the boardwalk and climbed up on his horse. He gave the men a salute, then trotted down the road back to Miller's Pond. When he'd left the wagon train, the ladies were up to their necks in the pond giving their bodies and hair a good scrubbing. He could tell from the excited chatter they couldn't wait to start their new lives.

The next morning, the wagon train moved slowly toward town. When they reached the edge of Sunflower, Slim had the ladies drive the wagons into a wide circle with all the cows, extra horses and mules secured in the center. Since all the ladies were cleaned and dressed in their best finery, Tate's men unhitched the horses and mules and placed them in the circle with the others.

Jeremy brought around a big flatbed wagon for the ladies to

ride to the big barn at the edge of town. Slim, Jeremy and a couple of the other men, helped the ladies onto the wagon. They were as quiet as a rabbit near a coyote. If a person didn't know any better, he would have thought the ladies were headed to a funeral instead of a big gala held in their honor.

In front of the big red barn stood an assortment of men—tall, short, good-looking and ugly. All were dressed in their Sunday best with their beards neatly trimmed and hair slicked down with tonic. Gone was the excitement. Now they appeared to be lined up for a firing squad.

Tate and Elly watched as the ladies were helped off the wagon and formed a semicircle across from the men. The sheriff stepped forward and welcomed the women to Sunflower, Texas, and their new home.

Tate stepped beside the sheriff and said that after studying everyone's wishes for a new wife, Miss Eddy had chosen a proper mate for each one. "She will now call out each couple's names. Now as I told the sheriff, this meeting is not a lifetime commitment. You will have this afternoon to get acquainted, and if your personality or desires are not to either party's satisfaction, there will be no hard feelings and you do not have to marry. Do I make myself clear?"

A few men grumbled, but no one walked away.

"Now, when Miss Eddy calls out your names, join your partner and go inside the barn for refreshments." Tate said as he stepped back beside the sheriff.

Elly stepped forward. "Gentlemen, I read and studied your wishes as I did the ladies. I pray that I have chosen well for each of you. The first couple is Martha Little and Jake Smallwood." Many cheers went up as Jake took Martha's hand. He bowed to her and placed her arm in the crook of his and walked into the barn. Both of them were smiling.

"The next couple is Lillian White and Jared Miller." A lovely young girl with long brown hair and sparkling eyes stepped up to a handsome man with sandy hair and deep dimples. Both of them reached out at the same time and took hands. More cheers shattered the quiet as the lovely couple disappeared into the barn. Elly continued to call couple after couple until everyone was matched with a partner.

Elly watched as Mattie held the hand of her new companion—Bill Sawyer, a handsome farmer who was well-established in the community. Little Johnny trailed behind them with a lonesome expression on his face.

"Well, Miss Eddy, you have done a fine job, and I am pleased with how everything is going. It looks to me like the preacher will perform many weddings this afternoon," Mr. Maynard said. "So, Tate, have you told Miss Elly that this is our last trip and that we'll be settling here on our ranch?"

Before Tate could reply, Elly asked. "Mercy, I had no idea you would be giving up your business. What made you to decide to retire, I guess I should say?"

"Honey, look at me. I'm older than dirt, and these old bones are ready to settle down in one place. Tate has agreed to live here and raise cattle and a family. We have planned this for many years, and now it's time," he said, with a contented expression on his rough cheeks. "So, Miss Elly, what are your plans now that we have arrived in this nice town? Since you chose not to be one of the brides, have you given much thought to how you're going to support yourself?"

"I had thought about teaching school, but since I don't have a teacher's certificate, they don't have to pay me a decent salary. Maybe I can find something else to do. I want to help Mrs. Duffy get settled, but if I can't find a job, I'll have to move on."

"Well, I'm sure something will turn up. Speaking for myself, I would hate for you to leave Sunflower since you just arrived here. Please remember that I will be as close as our ranch, if you ever need anything." With a tip of his Stetson, he turned and strolled toward the barn to join in the celebration.

Elly picked up her papers and notes that she had used to help make her selections and walked toward town, having no idea where she was going to stay the night. She sighed and bit her bottom lip to keep the tears at bay. As she stepped upon the boardwalk, Mrs. Duffy came out of the abandoned house on the end of the street.

"Oh, Elly, here you are. I want you to meet Mr. Flowers. He owns this old place, and he says that it once was a boardinghouse and it's for sale. Can you believe it? I think its fate." She smiled at Elly and took her hands in her small ones. "May I show my friend the inside of the house, Mr. Flowers? I'll lock the door behind us and bring you the key. Will you be at the dance?"

"Certainly, Mrs. Duffy. You take all the time you need and just bring the key to my office in the morning." He lifted his hat and wished both of the ladies a good evening.

"Come inside and see what a wonderful old house this is. I know it needs some repairs, but the fireplaces all work and the big stove in the kitchen is in good working order. The stairs need repaired in some places but there are five rooms upstairs and a water closet in each room. On the bottom floor, there are three rooms and a big water closet with several large tubs for bathing. There's room in there to hang clothes to dry when needed. I just love this place. What do you think?" Out of breath, she circled the room.

"I love this cozy-looking parlor off the dining area. Is that the kitchen in the back?" She entered through the swinging door, and a smile broke out on her face. "Oh Mrs. Duffy, I love this large kitchen. You could place a table in that corner and serve breakfast to some of your patrons who need to eat early."

"Elly, do you think that I could make a living here in this big house? It is a little bigger than the one in Leesville, but I'm not sure if Sunflower has a need for a big rooming house."

"With the nice parlor, you might could offer to hold parties here, maybe special meetings, or even weddings. Oh, we could fix the room up so inviting that everyone who came to town would want to stop in for tea and . . . pie. I can bake pies." Elly swung Mrs. Duffy around.

"Oh, what a wonderful idea. I will need help with cooking and cleaning for our guests. You will just have to move in with me. You can live on the bottom floor next to me, and this will solve your problem as to where you will live and work."

"Are you sure? You could rent my room and bring in more money."

"I can't serve food and special pies for guests in this big house all by my lonesome, if all the rooms are rented," she said laughing as she waltzed around the room. "Tomorrow, I'll go see Mr. Flowers and make a deal with him. Maybe Mr. Maynard will go with me and help me make an offer."

"Now that sounds like a plan. Where do you suppose we'll spend the night?" Elly asked.

"I figured we would stay one more night in our wagon. I'm sure Mr. Maynard will let us. Besides, the ladies have to remove their items out of the wagons," Mrs. Duffy said. "Let's go to the dance and have a nice chat with him."

Chapter 14

Mattie met Elly when she entered the barn. The music was loud and everyone seemed to be having a grand time. She smiled at Mattie, then at Johnny as he clung to his sister's skirt.

"What's wrong, Mattie," Elly leaned close and whispered. "You're as white as a sheet. Where is your new groom-to-be?"

"I am sorry, but I can't marry that . . . man. He's drunk, and I hate a man who drinks. He's a mean drunk, too."

Elly stiffened at her words. Memories of her pa being drunk—the loud swearing, staggering in the door, and making demands on her mama came roaring back to her.

Mattie grabbed her arm. "Elly, please help me. I won't marry that man. He says that I have baby-making hips, and he's going to keep me with child so he can have many field hands. He told Johnny he couldn't go to school because he'd be too busy working the fields from sunup to dark. When Johnny said he wanted to go to school, he raised his hand to strike him. If I hadn't jumped in front of my brother, he would have hit him. A child, Elly, he would have hit a small child."

"Mercy, Mattie. Of course, you don't have to marry that drunk. I am so sorry. On his application he said he loved children and wanted many. I thought because he loved them, he would be happy to have Johnny. Oh, Lord, please forgive me."

"It's not your fault, but I ain't going to marry a man who will be mean to my brother," she said and fell into Elly's arms crying.

"Come on, woman. Let's get in line and get hitched so we can head home," Bill Sawyer called to Mattie as he staggered over to both ladies.

Elly forced Mattie behind her and stepped in front of her and little Johnny. "Mr. Sawyer, I hate to tell you this, but Mattie is not going to marry you tonight or any time. You have proven to her that you're not the right person she should marry. Why don't you go and drink some coffee while I get your fifty dollars from Tate Maynard?"

"Well, Miss, if that little bitch don't want to marry me, that's fine. You'll do just fine as her replacement. You're a hell of a lot prettier." He grasped at Elly's wrist so fast she didn't have time to jump back.

"Come on," he demanded and jerked Elly nearly off her feet. "The preacher is waiting and I'm in need of a—" Before Mr. Sawyer got the filthy words out of his mouth, Tate's fists met Sawyer's mouth and knocked him onto his back.

"Hey man, why'd you do that?" Mr. Sawyer rubbed his chin, then spat blood out of his mouth.

Tate reached into his pocket and pulled out a handful of green bills and flung them on the ground in front of the man. "There's your refund for a bride. You aren't fit to marry one of my ladies."

"What's going on here, Mr. Maynard?" Sheriff Murray joined the large circle of people forming around them.

"This fellow needs to sober up and learn some manners. He won't be standing in line to get married any time soon."

"Come on, Sawyer. I see you've been hitting the bottle again. A good night in my small hotel will be just the thing for you." Sheriff Murray motioned for two men to help him up off the ground and escort him to the jailhouse.

"Thanks, Sheriff. I hope the ladies won't have any more

trouble out of him."

"He'll be sober tomorrow and head back to his farm," Sheriff Murray said. "All right, folks, the show's over. Get back inside and enjoy the rest of the party."

Tate watched Elly for a few minutes. She hugged Mattie and Johnny, reassuring them that everything would be fine. "Elly's right, Miss Mattie. You and Johnny are welcome to stay in your wagon tonight. My pa will help you get settled in town tomorrow."

"Thank you, Mr. Maynard. I was so afraid, but I'll take my future in my hands and try to make a good life here in Sunflower for both of us." She took her little brother's hand and went back inside the barn.

Tate sidled up next to Elly and gave her a shadow of a smile. He took her hand and pulled her away from the light of the barn and the sound of loud music.

"Where you dragging me to, Mr. Ex-Boss Man?"

"Thank the good Lord," Tate said. "I'm happy not to be responsible for you any longer. You and you alone have given me fits on this long trip. I'm glad we got here with you in one piece," he said with almost a smile on his face." Maybe that old man, Mr. Williams, was right when he said you were a jinx."

"How dare you!" Elly said and jerked her hand loose from his. "I can't help that bad things happen to me."

"Really? The fight between me and that drunken jerk would not have taking place if you had come and gotten me, but no, you had to take him on by yourself. A drunk twice your size." He had stooped down at eye level with her, mere inches from her nose.

"I was paid to take care of the brides, Mr. Know-it-all." Elly sidestepped him and whirled away, mumbling under her breath how she'd like to do him bodily harm.

Tate demanded that she stand still, then spun her around to face him. She glared at him like a mama wildcat ready to protect her cubs. With narrowed eyes, he clasped both of his big hands on her slim shoulders and pulled her toward his body. The kiss he planted over her lips was possessive and laid claim to what he wanted more than anything in the world.

A wave of desire flowed through Elly as her knees nearly folded. His kiss enflamed her body from her head to her toes. She felt on fire, lost in his masculine scent as he lifted her arms and placed them easily around his neck.

Elly knew she was standing out in the street, kissing a man she would love to pound into the ground, but she was too weak to resist his arms. When his hold on her body loosened, she could barely catch her breath. "Let me go, Tate. I can't seem to fight you, even though I know you don't care for me," she whispered as his arms fell from her trembling body.

"Elly, listen—" but she twisted away from him and ran toward the wagon train.

Tate stood and watched her race away with a look of annoyance on his face. What was he going to do about this woman who got under his rough hide every minute of every day?

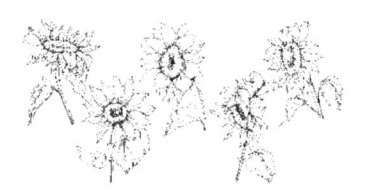

Chapter 15

Early the next morning, Mrs. Duffy and Major Maynard stepped onto the boardwalk laughing. Mrs. Duffy waved the deed to her new rooming house. With Major's presence and knowledge of the town, Mrs. Duffy was able to purchase the rooming house with her lifesavings and forego a mortgage. "I will always have a roof over my head and I won't have to worry about making a payment to the bank each month." Mrs. Duffy hugged the major and patted his back. "Whenever you're in town, my table is always open to you."

"Now, that's an invitation I will gladly accept," he replied as they stopped in front of her new building. "Here you are. Your new home."

"You know, Major, this will be Elly's new home, too. That young girl's going to live with me and help me with my boarders by cooking and cleaning. She will be baking pies for my guests and hopes to sell some to the café down the street. I'm so happy to have her stay with me."

"This is good news to me, too. I was going to talk with her today and see if she'd made any plans. She's a lovely, smart girl, and a man would be mighty lucky to catch her for his bride." He took her hand and squeezed it. "Take care and be sure to let me know if I can help you in any way. Tate and I will be selling our wagons and rounding up the animals to take to our ranch soon. I'll let you know when we're leaving town."

"I'm disappointed we'll not see you and your son every day, but I understand you have a big ranch outside of town. I know you've looked forward to settling down and not having to travel anymore."

"I'll see you before we move out to the ranch. Good day, fair lady," A sweet smile crossed his face, then he walked away.

Mrs. Duffy went inside her new boarding house. She went from room to room while waiting for Elly to come with their things. She opened the back door, then decided to prop the front door open and allow the cross breeze to flow through the house. When she bent to pick up a flowerpot large enough to hold the door, she noticed Tate standing in the middle of the street talking with Elly. Oh, my goodness, she thought. They look like they're arguing again. As she turned to go back inside, a blast of gunfire sounded, then a big black horse raced down the middle of the hard-packed road.

A look of concern spread over Tate's face. "Pa and I will be going to our ranch this morning. I don't want to leave you here—alone. I can't help but be worried about what you're going to do."

"That's sweet of you to be concerned about me, but as you know, I'm a big girl and I have taken take of myself for years. I don't need you worrying about me." Before she could tell him she would be living and working with Mrs. Duffy, he stomped his foot like a child.

"Now, I know exactly how you take care of yourself. You're always getting in the middle of—" Tate didn't finish his sentence. With the blast of the gun, his body fell forward into Elly's arms. Blood flowed from a hole in his shirt as they both slid to the ground.

She heard Major call Tate's name, but his body pinned her underneath. "Help," Elly screamed, but her voice was muffled. The footsteps and shouts of men came from the store and the saloon. Warm liquid seeped over her. Tate's blood.

"Get the doctor," she screamed.

"Help me, men." Major dropped to the ground beside his son. "Let's get him in the rooming house out of the street. The doctor can care for him better in a bed." He sobbed, "Oh Lord, please don't take my son. He's such a good man, and his life is just beginning. Please, let him live. He's all I have to live for," Major kept praying as the men helped carry Tate into the rooming house.

Elly pulled herself up and followed them in. Mrs. Duffy held the door open for her, then tossed clean sheets over a mattress in a room off from the kitchen. "Put him here," Mrs. Duffy said. "I have some hot water on the stove and I'll get some clean rags." She looked at Elly, her eyes traveling to the blood on her shirt, face and neck. "Are you hurt, child? Were you shot?"

"No, I'm not hurt. This blood is Tate's. He fell into my arms and we tumbled to the ground. I need to cut Tate's shirt and see how bad he's hurt before the doctor gets here. Please bring the water and clean rags so I can stop the flow of blood."

"Miss, we have him settled on the bed," A tall young man in overalls said. He carried a straw hat in his hands.

Elly had begun to cut Tate's shirt when a man calling himself Doc Weaver came in the room. "Good, woman. Open my bag and pull out a needle while I look him over." As he poked around on Tate's shoulder, Elly asked, "Aren't you going to wash your hands before you treat him?"

"Of course, pour water over my hands now. Give me a clean towel," he said as he peered at her over his wire-rimmed glasses. He dried his hands, reached into his bag and pulled out a vial labeled *Morphine*. He filled the needle with the medicine and stuck Tate with it. "This will help with the pain while I remove the gunpowder particles. He's lucky. The bullet missed the bone. It went through his back and out the front shoulder."

"Are you going to operate here, now?" Elly asked.

"Yes, I need your help, but if you can't stand the sight of blood, get out and send that old woman in here."

"I can help. Tell me what to do." Elly held her chin up and swallowed hard.

"All right, let's get him on his side. Maybe you should stand and hold him while I pour this whiskey on the wound."

"Won't that hurt him—burn, I mean?"

"Hell, it would if he was awake. I've got to disinfect the area where I'm going to poke around for any fragments of the bullet. I got to get the hole clean." After thirty minutes, the doctor sewed him up and placed a bandage over the wound. He washed his hands and rolled down his shirt sleeves. "If Tate gets an infection, his arm may have to be amputated," the old doctor said matter-of-factly.

"No," Elly shrieked at the doctor, making him jump. "You will not cut his arm off while I have breath in my body. I will take excellent care of him."

"Good, he will need constant care for a few weeks. I can't sit with him twenty-four hours a day. His pa can help you some, but changing his bandages need to be done by you." The doctor closed his bag. "I'll leave some pain medicine for him. Only give it to him as needed."

The sheriff came into the kitchen of the rooming house. He walked over to Major who sat bent over in a chair with his eyes closed and his head bowed.

"I'm sorry, Major, but Bill Sawyer got away. I'll send out a telegram to the marshal in the next town. He'll post a wanted poster on him for attempted murder." Shaking his head, he continued. "I let him out this morning and he said that he was headed back to his farm. He never gave me a clue he was mad or wanted to get back at Tate for the argument they had last night."

"Thanks, Murray. That fool has just made a simple argument into a very bad situation for himself. I appreciate what you've done already. Let's pray that Elly and the doctor can take care of Tate, and that the good Lord will heal him." Major hung his head and walked into the room where Elly was washing the blood off Tate's chest and arms.

"Oh good, Major. Will you help me remove your son's pants and boots?" Elly asked. "And I'd like for you to bring him some clean underthings. He's going to be here for a while, and I need to keep him as clean as possible."

After they removed his pants and covered his body, Major left to get the items that Elly had requested. He was pleased to know that this sweet girl was going to care for his son. He had watched the couple work closely together on the trip to Sunflower. Tate had strong feelings for Elly but he tried hard not to show it.

"Miss Elly, I need to go out to our ranch with my men and get settled. Do you think it would be wise of me to leave Tate?" Major asked. "I'll send his clothes and personal items back by one of my men. I'm so sorry to have to drop this responsibility on you. Tate would never want you to feel that you have to care for him."

"I feel responsible. That man was mad at Tate because of me." Elly frowned. "Listen, please go to your ranch. Your son is going to be asleep for a day or two for sure. When he wakes, I'm sure he's going to be in pain, so after more medicine, he'll go right back to sleep. Sleep is good. I'll take good care of him."

"I'll be back in two or three days, but if I'm needed before then, send a man after me. We're only about seven miles from town." Major smiled at Elly and thanked her.

Dusk had fallen, and a gloom filled the bedroom as Elly stood over Tate's bed watching him sleep. His flailing arm hit her in the chest before she knew what happened. Clutching his hand, she studied his eyes to see if he was awake, but he wasn't. He was restless, probably feeling pain in his shoulder.

"You must lie still. Doctor's orders," she said and covered his good arm with the sheet. She felt his forehead and it felt cool, and for that she was thankful. Of course, less than twenty-four hours had passed since he was shot.

After Elly was sure he was sleeping soundly, she went to her room and dressed in her gown and robe. She told Mrs. Duffy she was going to sit in the rocker in Tate's room and watch over him during the night. As she read by a dim light, she guarded Tate. Time and time again, he tossed and tried to turn, but she ordered him to lie still. Exhausted, during the early hours of the morning, she laid her head down on his mattress and fell asleep with her face near his hip.

Tate felt hot. He tried to open his eyes, but bright sunlight shone directly on his face. Where was he? The last thing he remembered was arguing with Elly in the street. As he moved his leg, he felt something warm pressed up against his hip. He reached down and patted a handful of soft hair. Woman's hair. He raised his head and looked down at the woman. Wild black strands covered her face. Mercy, which hag from the Golden Nugget was lying in his bed?

As he shifted his body, a raw, burning pain surged through his torso. The upper top of his body was on fire. The pain was almost unbearable. What had happened to him? Was he dead and in hell? If he opened his eyes, would he awake from a nightmare and all his pain would disappear? He tried to swallow and open his eyelids, but he could do neither. Gritting his teeth until his jaw ached, he tried to raise his head, but the pain was too great. He slipped back into oblivion. In the depth of darkness, he kept hearing commands from a faraway voice. "Open your mouth, roll over, don't roll over, be still, go back to sleep." He tried hard to ignore the monster's demands.

Miserable and aching all over, Elly quietly rose from the bed and went into the kitchen for a much-needed cup of coffee. Sleeping with her head on the mattress, bent over while sitting in the rocker, made her back hurt so bad that she could hardly walk. She stretched and twisted her slim body to each side hoping to work the kinks out. The night had certainly taken a toll on her hair as well. She looked in the mirror as she pulled her hair out of her eyes and sighed. "Goodness, I look bad enough to scare myself."

After a good hot soak in the roomy water closet, she combed her hair and plaited it in a long rope. She put on a clean day dress similar to the one she'd worn the day before. Having only two, she'd have to wash them every night to stay clean.

A knock came from the door while Elly dressed. Maybe it was the doctor coming to check on Tate, she thought. Mrs. Duffy and another lady were speaking. Once Elly opened the door, she saw Mattie and Johnny sitting at the dining-room table. Mrs. Duffy excused herself and left the room.

"Oh, Mattie, it's so good to see you. I guess you heard that scoundrel you nearly married shot Tate. The sheriff let him out of jail to go home, but he got liquored up again, I guess. Thank the good Lord his aim was off when he shot at Tate."

"Miss Elly, I understand that he could have shot you too," Mattie said, her voice full of concern.

"Heavens," Elly said. "I never gave it any thought that he might have been shooting at me instead of Tate. We may never know the answer. I just know he rushed from the buildings and shot Tate before we could move out of the street. I've never been so scared. Tate isn't out of danger yet."

"If I can help take care of him, I'd be happy to do whatever I can. Johnny can help by running errands for you. There isn't much work in this town for a single woman," Mattie said, her eyes on the floor. "Well, I could work at the Golden Nugget Saloon, but I could have done that back in Leesville."

Mrs. Duffy piped in from the kitchen. "I got an idea."

Both girls turned to face her.

"Sorry, I was eavesdropping. C'mon in the kitchen. I got up early and bought enough food to fill the pantry. I'm making soup."

They joined her in the kitchen where Mrs. Duffy was chopping vegetables.

"Mattie, how would you and Johnny like to come and live here with me and Elly. I need someone to help me clean rooms, serve the food, and wash up after each meal. Elly is going to have her hands full for the next couple of weeks taking care of young Mr. Maynard. I can't pay you much until I start getting people to board here and take their meals. I'm hoping to offer hot meals to people who live here in town as well as the travelers on the stagecoach. The café only serves sandwiches and sweets. The men will appreciate having a home-cooked meal once in a while. What do you think?"

"Are you saying I can live here and work for you and earn a little money?" She hurried on with another question. "Can Johnny live with us?"

"Now Mattie, I included Johnny in my invitation to you. Of course he can live with us. I'm crazy about the little fellow, and I was already missing him." Johnny ran over and gave her a big hug around the waist.

Mattie rushed into Mrs. Duffy's arms. "Oh, Mrs. Duffy, you are an answer to my prayers. The school is down the street and he can walk there every morning."

"Yes," he chimed in, but Elly placed her hand over his small mouth. "We must be quiet while Mr. Maynard is resting."

"I know he was shot. Is he going to die?" Johnny asked.

"Not if I can help it. We're all going to take real good care of him. Will you help do things for him if I ask?"

"Yes, madam. I like Mr. Maynard lots, and I will help you get him well."

"Mattie, are your things still in the wagon?" Elly asked.

"No, I have all my things stacked up against the wall on the side of this building. The ladies had to remove everything out of the wagons early this morning."

"Good, let's go bring your things inside and get you settled so you can start helping us get this place in shape for boarders. Mrs. Duffy, will you listen out for Tate, please."

"Of course I will. Johnny, you go with your sister and Miss Elly and help them bring your things into your new home."

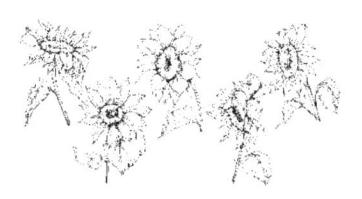

Chapter 16

Early the next morning, Elly touched Tate's forehead and it felt hot. She prepared a bowl of vinegar water and bathed his face, neck and chest. She continued with the cool water until he seemed to relax. The doctor would hopefully come early and check his bandages. Fever usually meant infection, and she was going to do everything in her power to keep it down. As if on cue, someone pounded on the front door. "It's Doc Weaver."

"My goodness, old man, you don't have to knock so loud. No one here is deaf, and we have a sick man trying to sleep." Mrs. Duffy grumbled loud enough for everyone to hear as she led the doctor into Tate's room.

Elly glanced up from Tate's bedside. "I'm so happy to see you this morning, doctor. I'm afraid Mr. Maynard is getting a fever. His forehead was hot to the touch, but I've been giving him cool baths with vinegar water to help lower it."

"That's just the thing, young woman. Help me check the bandages. I hope the stitches have held. Has he tried to move around while sleeping?"

"Some, but I held him tight," Elly explained.

The old doc raised his gray eyebrows. "That's a good girl. He needs to be made to lie still."

The doctor removed the first layer of bandages from Tate's shoulder and back. The medicine had not worn off, but he still moaned from pain. Elly flinched every time a sound came from Tate and cringed while the doctor examined his body. He continued poking around the wounds and rewrapped them with clean bandages. Both dried and fresh blood stained the old ones.

"I didn't see any infection setting in yet, but keep wiping him with cool cloths if he's hot. I expect he'll be waking up soon hungry as a bear. Only give him broth and a lot of water. Nothing else until I give you permission. He'll be cross and demanding, but do as I say. He'd only throw up if he eats or drinks, and I don't want him busting those stitches open." He snapped his black doctor's bag closed. "Don't let him out of bed either. That's the first thing he'll try to do."

"Doctor Weaver, would you like to have some breakfast? Mattie and I have prepared some food. I'm going to serve early risers in the kitchen, but later people will be served in the dining room."

"What a nice idea, Madam, but I have to get on the road and check on a patient who nearly lost his leg yesterday. Like Miss Eddy here, his wife is caring for him and I know she's worried. I would enjoy your offer another morning. Thank you." He tipped his hat and slipped out the door.

Elly had left Tate sleeping quietly. Just as she poured herself a fresh cup of coffee, the springs in his mattress creaked. She hurried back to the room to find him trying to pull himself up against the headboard.

"Goodness, Tate, you can't sit up yet, especially by yourself. You're going to bust all your stitches loose. Now lie back down carefully."

"What . . . what happened to me?" He frowned at his raspy voice.

"While you and I were in the street chatting yesterday morning,

Bill Sawyer rode by us and shot you. Thank the good Lord the bullet went all the way through your shoulder and out the back. Doc Weaver operated on you. You have a small hole in your back but a bigger wound on the front of your right shoulder where the bullet came out. Doc said you'll be fine if you follow his instructions. After Doc Weaver assured your pa you're going to be all right, your pa went out to your ranch for a few days and left you in my care." She felt as if she was rattling on, but he only stared at her.

"I've got to relieve myself. Get me some pants and help me up."

"No, you cannot get up. I'll get you a pail to use. Can you manage by yourself or do . . . I mean . . . I'll get Johnny to help you. Be right back." Before she turned to leave, she pointed a teacher finger at him. "Don't you dare move an inch."

Pain like no other shot through Tate's body as he shifted to one side of the bed. After he settled back on the mattress, he felt like he'd been shot again.

Elly prepared him a teaspoon of pain medicine with a small glass of water to chase it down.

"What's in that spoon?" he growled like a bear.

"Pain medicine. Open up, swallow quickly and drink this water."

"No, I hurt but I don't want to sleep. I want something to eat, now."

"Take this medicine and I'll get you food," she said.

"No, food first and then maybe . . . that." He pointed to the spoon filled with medicine.

"No, you can't sit up. Medicine, then food."

"Give me the damn stuff, then bring me ham and eggs and a gallon of hot coffee." He barked as she shoveled the spoon into his mouth, "Oh, damnit . . . what's that . . . stuff?" He slurred his words and shuddered all over.

"Some medicine that will help you get well soon," Elly replied. "Lie still, please, while I prepare your food."

As she left the room, he tried to get comfortable. He closed his eyes, and in just a few minutes, he was out of pain and in a deep sleep.

Elly tiptoed to the entrance of his room and grinned. The medicine worked fast and he rested again. The doctor was right about him being a bear. Goodness, she thought, I hope he'll soon be in a better mood and cooperate with me.

Mrs. Duffy and Mattie were busy preparing lunch. A rich vegetable soup and cornbread were on the menu with apple pie for dessert. She would spoon some of the broth in a cup to feed Tate when he woke up.

Both ladies were busy sweeping and dusting the dining room and parlor. All the furniture was shining from the beeswax used on the tables and chairs. A bouquet of wildflowers had been placed in the center of the table on top of a white tablecloth that Mrs. Duffy had discovered in a closet. The place had taken on a homey atmosphere in just one day.

Later, Mrs. Duffy announced she and Mattie would start on the upstairs rooms. She had opened all the windows to let in fresh air. The bed linens were soaking in a big pot out on the back porch. Afterwards, they would be hung on the two lines that were stretched from one tree to another with tall poles to hold them up high. With the sun so bright and hot, all the linens would be ready to be placed on the beds before nightfall.

The last owner had abandoned the building to be sold as is. He didn't bother to take any of the nice things in the house, which was an added bonus for Mrs. Duffy. Each room had a pretty ceramic bowl and pitcher, a working lantern and scarves on all the furniture. All the windows had roll-up shades, but none of the rooms had curtains. Each room had a desk with a straight-back chair, which gave the room a nice touch.

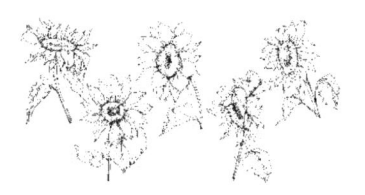

Chapter 17

By last afternoon, Tate became the bear the doctor had warned her about. Elly had fled from Tate's room, and all of her so-called calm expressions had left her completely. She wanted to scream at her unruly patient. He was disrespectful and didn't care how he talked to a lady.

He leaned forward and yelled through the doorway. "Get your fanny back in here. I am not finished with you yet."

Elly summoned her strength, hurried back into the room and ordered him to shut his ill-mannered mouth before she told him a thing a two about his conduct.

"Oh really, Miss Smart Mouth, why don't you just tell me how you really feel. Don't hold back anything. I'm a big boy. I can take whatever abuse you sling at me." His challenging blue eyes locked with hers. "I'm waiting, your highness."

She met his gaze. If the daggers in her eyes could have killed, he would be a dead goose. She balled her hands into fists, and her body shook from anger. How she wished she could explain to him about her childhood and how her papa had mistreated her mama. How he had walked away from the house and never came back, leaving her mama to support two children. At least the abuse had stopped, but no man was ever going to manhandle her and force her to do his bidding.

Elly swallowed the bile that had risen in her throat. "Leave me alone, you big dumb ox, before I say something we both regret." He'd made her so mad she was sick to her stomach. She had to get away from this brute before she said words that would be hard to take back. Well he asked for it, she thought, before he grabbed her and twisted her wrist. Elly ran out of the room, to his loud laughter.

She plopped down on the front porch and closed her eyes. The sunny breeze felt nice against her cheeks. Fall was near but the shorter days were still hot. Today she didn't care. Large puffs of white clouds floated by at top speed. Were they going to have another summer storm? Sighing she stood and looked down the street at the other stores. A few people walked in and out of the dry goods store and a couple of old men sitting at the end of the boardwalk played checkers.

With her head filled with Tate's troubles, she went back inside the parlor. The house was quiet except for Tate's snoring. Thank you, Lord, she thought. She needed to take the opportunity and rest while he was sleeping peacefully.

After Tate had awakened from his long nap, he was in a lighthearted mood. He laughed as he thought about his little romp with Elly. She could give as well as he could, and that made life enjoyable.

Chapter 18

Elly stood in front of a kitchen mirror. She twisted her head one way and then another to get a full view of her long hair. How she wished she had a nice hat to wear to the church service this morning.

"Where do you think you're marching off to? Have you forgotten I have to eat?" Tate watched her from his bed.

"You've had your breakfast, sir," Elly said with a smile.

"You call that piss you brought in here two hours ago food? I told you I wanted ham and eggs with a half dozen of those fluffy biscuits."

"Sorry . . . until the doctor says you can have solid food, that is all I'm allowed to give you. Maybe tomorrow he'll allow me to feed you something else."

"You didn't answer my question. Where in the hell are you going that you have to primp for hours in front of a mirror?"

"Mr. Maynard, you must clean up your language and be the nice man I first met on the wagon train. And to answer your question, I'm going to church to pray for your soul." Elly shouldered her bag and reached for her Bible. "We'll be back in a couple of hours. Why don't you take a nap, and I'll feed you lunch when I return."

"Who's going to stay here and take care of me?" he yelled loud enough for the congregation at the church to hear him. Elly didn't even bother to give him an answer. Tate didn't really want anyone taking care of him. He was just being his arrogant self.

Mrs. Duffy agreed to stay home and continued cooking a big lunch. She'd mentioned that she hoped some of the townspeople would come by for a meal. Mattie had painted a sign and nailed it on the front of the rooming house. Elly had placed a handwritten sign on the post office and telegraph wall advertising the meals and cost.

Tate tried to stay in bed and rest, but his stomach growled. He could feel his backbone rubbing against his stomach. "Mrs. Duffy," Tate called. "I need something to eat, please," he yelled and then softened his tone. "Elly won't feed me anything, but I've got to have food. She's starving me."

"Now, Mr. Maynard, Elly is only following the doctor's orders. Doc Weaver is afraid your stomach will reject the food and you'll rip your stitches when you start throwing up. Please don't blame Elly. She's been so upset over you being shot and feels responsible that you got hurt by that awful man."

"That's crazy. She didn't make that fool shoot me."

"I'll bring you a cup of hot broth with a few pieces of chicken in it and a nice piece of soft bread. Just lie still and I'll bring it in to you." Mrs. Duffy disappeared out the door.

Elly and Mattie came into the house laughing. Mattie told Johnny to go and change into his play clothes. "Lay your good clothes on the bed, and I'll put them away for next Sunday," she said, while tying a white apron over her Sunday dress.

"Sounds like you enjoyed the church service this morning. I can't wait to go next week."

Mattie laughed. "Oh, Mrs. Duffy, Elly was the center of attention in church. The men couldn't listen to the sermon for watching her. After the service, she was surrounded by men and one of them proposed to her. I wish you had seen him." Mattie couldn't contain her laughter. "He pulled her away from the other men and practically begged her to be his mail-order bride. As wide as a barn door and redder than a fresh, raw beet, he stuttered, but with his pa's help, he got it out."

"His pa helped with the proposal? Mercy, Elly. Who was this man?" Mrs. Duffy asked.

"He was a nice young man—an enormous man," she commented and laughed. "I would never have to fear anything if he was around. Oh, my goodness, Mattie, the other men are still standing in the parlor." Elly knew that she should go and sit with them at the dining table, but she needed to care for Tate. "Tell them we have chicken and dumplings, roast beef with potatoes, carrots and green beans, and red beans and sausages."

"Goodness, this is a feast. With biscuits, corn bread and hot peach cobbler, we may never get rid of this bunch," Mattie said as she went to greet and seat the men.

"Elly!" Tate called from his doorway. "Get your skinny behind in here, now."

"I guess my good morning is over," mumbled Elly as she placed an apron over her blue calico dress.

What is this I hear about some big ox asking her to marry him? If she marries anyone it will be me. Where did that idea come from? "Who is he?" Tate asked as he rubbed the dark stubble on his face. He couldn't believe how jealous he felt, knowing that other men were sniffing out Elly.

"It's not any of your business. Besides, I am not interested in marrying anyone, and you of all people know that." She straightened his covers, then noticed the empty cup of chicken broth. "I see Mrs. Duffy has fed you your lunch. I guess she gave you some bread and the broth was probably full of chicken pieces," she said as she viewed the cup.

"She did and it was wonderful. That was just to hold me over until you got home. I want a big bowl of those dumplings and a half dozen buttered biscuits."

"Maybe, if Doc Weaver comes over here for lunch. I'm sure he'll come in and check you over. Maybe, just maybe, he will allow you to sit up some."

"I don't give a damn about sitting up. I want food and I want it now." He demanded as he tried to shift his legs around on the bed.

Johnny stuck his head in. "Miss Elly, that old man is at the door. Can he come into the kitchen to see you?"

"Yes," said Tate and Elly at the same time. Johnny glanced at both of the adults. "I'll get him." He ran out of the room and returned with the old doc, dressed in a long black coat although the temperature outside neared ninety.

"This old rooming house has never smelled so good," Doc Weaver said as he entered Tate's room. "I can't wait to put my feet under that table."

"I want to eat, too. Just think how I feel lying here having to smell the wonderful food cooking and can't have any. Tell that grumpy gatekeeper of yours I can have some solid food. I'm starving to death," Tate demanded.

"All right, all right, let me have a look at your wounds. Have they been bleeding, Miss Elly?' The doc opened his bag and took out a pair of sharp scissors.

"I haven't changed them since you were here yesterday morning."

"That's good. Any fever?" He pulled part of the bandage down and peeked at the wound.

"You can ask me your questions, Doc. I am not deaf and blind—yet."

"Well, I hope some solid food will change your disposition. You're as ornery as an old mule." The doc snapped his bag closed and turned to Elly. "Feed him a little solid food and he can get out of bed to walk to the water closet and maybe sit in the parlor for a little while. He'll let you know when he's ready for the bed." Turning to Tate, he peered over his thick spectacles. "Take it slow, young man, or I will report you to your pa. I stopped at your ranch yesterday and he said he was coming into town today. I'll be by tomorrow."

Mrs. Duffy met him at the patient's door. He patted his stomach. "I'm ready to partake of a meal at your table today if you have room for me. I cannot believe some of those boys are actually having lunch here."

"Oh," Mrs. Duffy smiled. "They followed Elly home from church. They're all trying to win her hand in matrimony." She giggled and told him about the big country boy proposing to her after church.

"Well, looks like we might just have a real wedding pretty soon," he said loud enough for Tate and Elly to hear. Mrs. Duffy took his arm and led him out of Tate's room.

"Don't just stand there, woman. Get me some real food and be quick about before I have to hire myself a real nurse."

Tate's angry words cut to the quick. Elly whirled around and hurried to the kitchen. She grabbed a bowl and flopped a big spoonful of hot dumplings in it and placed two large biscuits on top. She raced into the room and set the tray on the nightstand. "Here, you insufferable pig. Enjoy it because that's all you're getting until supper." Elly left the room and returned with a hot wet washcloth. She hit him square in the face with it. "Most pigs like to be clean before they eat."

"You mean raccoons, not pigs, don't you?" Tate yelled at her retreating backside and guffawed. He took the clean cloth and wiped his face and hands. The warm water felt so good. He wanted a full tub of steaming water next. Just thinking about Elly having to bathe him made him feel better already.

Satisfied, and without as much pain as before, Tate waited patiently for Elly to return and ask if he needed anything else. She could be headstrong, but she was taking excellent care of him. After waiting for what seemed like an hour, he needed to go down the hall to the water closet. His patience had worn thin, but by the time she entered his room, she looked flushed and her hair had pulled loose from her pins on one side.

"It's about time you showed up. You look like you've had a romp with some cowboy. Who is the unlucky guy?" He said with a cocky grin on his face.

"How dare you—" Elly's face turned flaming red. "I'll have you know that I have been helping in the dining room. We've had over twenty people show up for lunch, and as soon as someone completed their meal, another sat down. I can't believe you haven't heard all the noise. If business keeps up, we're going to have to serve people at the kitchen table."

"When you say "we," do you mean Mrs. Duffy's business?"

"Yes. Mattie and I are both working and living here, too. She wants me to be her partner, buy into the business, but Mattie is just staying until she marries."

"Mrs. Duffy knows you haven't got a dime to your name. How can she expect you to 'buy into her business' as you put it," Tate asked.

"She said that I can work for her and draw a minimum salary, and the rest goes into my partnership."

"So, you'll work your fingers to the bone, receive a pence a week, and hope you'll live long enough to be her partner in this rundown building."

"You make it sound like I won't receive anything from her. At least, I'll have a roof over my head and three square meals a day."

"Damnit woman, a man in prison gets the same and he doesn't have to work as hard as you do." Tate swung his legs over the side of the bed. "I've got to pee. Help me or get out of my way."

"You are insufferable, you know that?"

"I've been called worse," he said grinning at her.

"Oh you," she smiled for the first time all day. "Place your good arm around my shoulders." Elly sat down on the bed and allowed Tate to adjust his good arm around her neck. They stood slowly at the same time. Step by step they made it down the hall to the water closet. As she started to enter the room, he placed his good arm across the open door. "This is as far as you go, little bird. I can do this part by myself," he said closing the door in her face.

Standing outside the water closet, Elly could hear Tate stumbling around. At least he had two good legs, but he was still as weak as a kitten. The door opened and he gave her a silly grin before he reached for her to help support his tall frame.

"If you would feed me a big steak tonight, it would help build up my blood, and I would get stronger more quickly."

"All right, you don't have to run a horse over me to get the message. A big juicy steak and a pile of fried potatoes for you tonight. But for now, rest. You need to take a nap. Plenty of rest is good medicine, too." Elly helped him lie down on the bed and she covered him with the top sheet.

"Thanks, sweetheart," he mumbled as he closed his eyes.

"Mercy," she said to Mattie after closing Tate's door. "Tate actually thanked me for the first time. What's this old world coming to?"

"You know he's crazy about you, don't you?" Mattie said as she peeled potatoes for the dinner meal.

"Now, Mattie, I know better. Tate puts up with me because he feels responsible for my welfare. His pa hired me to travel here and help with the brides on the trip, but they soon learned that I'm no farm girl. He tolerated me when he wasn't wringing my neck because of something stupid I did. We have never had a conversation without getting into an argument." Elly took a deep breath and looked at the closed bedroom door. "No, I'm afraid this is one time you and Mrs. Duffy are wrong."

Elly hung up her apron and retrieved her small handbag. "I'm going to the store and get a few things—mostly a big steak for Tate's supper tonight. Mrs. Duffy is serving pot roast and a big meatloaf for tonight's diners. That spice cake smells so good," Elly said as she went out the front parlor.

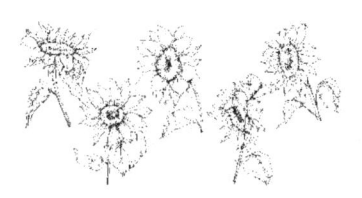

Chapter 19

Elly frowned at the few choices of meat old man Wilson had in the meat section of his store.

"Oh Miss Elly, why do you have that sad look on your face," Charles Hayes asked as he removed his gray Stetson. "I sure would like to help put a pretty smile back on your face by taking you to the little café and having a glass of cool lemonade."

"Oh, Mr. Hayes, that is awful nice of you, but I'm working. I came here to get a steak for my patient's supper this evening. He's weak and I'm trying to help him gain his strength back."

"Well, if you don't mind me saying so, if he can eat steak, I think he's well enough to take care of himself. I'd like to take care of you," he said grinning.

"Hello, Major," Elly said, thrilled beyond words to see him walking toward her. "When did you get into town? Have you visited with your son?"

"No, I only arrived a few minutes ago. I came in to get some tobacco before I go to the rooming house to see him. Are you ready to leave?"

"Let me get this piece of meat wrapped, and I'll walk with you. Just a minute, please."

"Howdy, Pole," Major spoke to Mr. Hayes.

"Howdy to you, sir," the six-foot-six man replied, then turned around. "Well Miss Elly, I'd best mosey along. Maybe we can talk again real soon." He tipped his hat and hurried out the door into the bright sunlight.

Elly sighed as she watched the gangly man disappear.

The major watched the interaction between the two of them. Elly seemed relieved that the young man had left the store. "Is that one of your new suitors, Miss Elly? I hope I didn't interrupt anything?"

"Are you kidding?" Mr. Wilson laughed loud. "That's just one of the many who are sniffing after her whenever she leaves the rooming house. She's had several marriage proposals, so I heard." He grinned, his eyes darting from Elly to Major.

"Mr. Wilson, that's not true. I've had only one proposal and it was nice, but I don't want to marry anyone," she said, peering up at Major.

After paying for her purchases, Major took her arm and strolled with her back to the rooming house. They peeked into Tate's room and saw that he was still resting.

"Come and sit and I will bring you coffee and a piece of Mattie's delicious spice cake," Elly instructed Major.

"How are you, Miss Mattie and little Johnny?" Major asked and pulled out a chair from the kitchen table.

"We are both doing well, thank you for asking. Johnny is in the first grade at school and he loves it. I'm so proud to be living close to the school so he can walk every morning with some of the other children. He's made a good friend already."

"That's mighty good to hear. He's a nice boy and I'm glad he's happy," he replied. "Speaking of being happy, I have come to take Tate home. I'm going to talk with the doc and make sure he can ride in the wagon. The ranch is only seven miles out of town."

"Who will care for him—change his bandages, help him in and out of bed?" Elly asked, her eyes locked on the closed bedroom door.

"Well, I was hoping you would come and spend the next week at our ranch and continue to nurse him. What do you think of that?"

"Why can't he just stay here?"

"Tate needs to get back to the ranch. We have correspondence and bills that need to be paid, and he has always been the businessman in the family. I need him to oversee these things while he's laid up for a while. He can also help instruct the men on how to handle the new ponies that were born while we were gone. There's nothing wrong with his legs, so he can walk around outside and get some fresh air."

"All that is true. He could do some of the things you mentioned, but he's still having a hard time with things since his right arm was hurt. I don't think he can write yet," she said.

"That's where you come in. You can take care of his wounds and help in the ranch office. I know he will appreciate having you with us."

Elly tossed her head back and laughed. "I'm not sure about that. We can't hardly be in the same room without arguing."

"Say you will come and help me care for Tate. One week, that's all I ask, please?"

"I will have to get someone to help Mrs. Duffy while I'm gone. This place has gotten so busy she needs Mattie and me helping all the time."

"Hello, anyone in the kitchen?" Tate called from behind his closed door.

"Major, our star patient is awake now. Go on in and talk with him. Afterward, I'll decide if I should go with you—for a few days."

Mrs. Duffy agreed that Elly should go to the ranch and

continue to help Tate with his recovery. Mrs. Langley, who worked for her daughter-in-law as a seamstress, was thrilled to get out of the back room of the shop and come and work at the rooming house. She sat in the rear of the shop near a window all day, never getting to visit with the customers. Her daughter-in-law was demanding and her only pay was room and board at their small house.

Tate was pleased to go home, but wasn't happy that Elly was still going to be his watchdog for another week. The doctor wouldn't let him go home without someone to care for him. "You'll need someone to help wash your wounds and change the bandages. I don't want any infection to set in, and if not kept clean, you could still lose your arm."

Tate gave in graciously and smiled as Elly climbed in the back of the wagon with him. She adjusted the sling that held his right arm like he was a child. Tate grunted but kept the stinging remark to himself. His pa had laid several quilts in the bed of the wagon while Tate leaned against the back of the buckboard.

"All right, children, we're homeward bound. Hold tight." Major's jolly mood was getting on Tate's nerves.

"Sorry, this is a rough ride. I'll try to be careful and not hit too many ruts."

Tate grunted and complained. "These boards hurt my back." He slid down on the quilts, trying to get comfortable.

"Here, lay your head in my lap, but be still." Elly adjusted her skirt so Tate could stretch out. His left hand weaseled its way under her skirt and before she knew it, his hand was under her chemise rubbing her thigh through her bloomers. Elly tried to rise, but he applied pressure on her leg, so she couldn't move.

"Take it easy, sweetheart. You don't want to hurt me right here behind my pa." His eyebrows bobbed and he patted her leg.

"One of these days, you're going to get what's coming to you," she said through gritted teeth.

Henry was standing on the back porch when Major drove the

wagon around to the back door. Jeremy Duke, the youngest ranch hand, raced from the barn and clasped the bridle of the lead horse while Major leaped to the ground.

"Come and help Tate and Elly down from the back of the wagon," he called to Slim.

"I don't need any damn help, Pa. I got two good legs." Tate gave Elly a warning look, then slid his bottom to the edge of the wagon and off the back to the ground. Pain shot through his shoulder, nearly causing his knees to buckle. Sweat beaded on his upper lip as he struggled to the back porch where Henry stood holding glasses of cold lemonade.

"I thought you might like a little refreshment after driving from town in this awful heat. Do you think it's ever going to get cool?" Henry smiled at Elly and handed her a big glass.

"It so nice to see you again, Henry. I'm happy to see someone I know this far from town." Elly took a big gulp of the refreshing drink. "This is wonderful."

Chapter 20

"Henry, where is Miguel's daughter I asked you to hire while I was gone to town? She was supposed to come and help you cook for us," Major asked.

"Well, it's like this. She ran off with a drifter. Left a note telling Miguel she was going to Mexico. He saddled up and left before daylight like a wild man. Said he was going to kill the man and drag his girl back home." Henry shook his head. "Now we're short a cook and a man to work the cattle while Miguel's gone."

Tate showed Elly her bedroom across the hall from his. She unpacked her carpetbag and opened two windows to allow a breeze to come into the room. The furniture was lovely. There was a large four-poster bed covered with a decorated quilt and two fluffy pillows next to the headboard. A rocking chair and small table holding a lantern sat next to the window. A dressing table with a mirror held a matching bowl and pitcher. Who decorated this big ranch house? After all, Tate and Major weren't married.

Elly's stomach growled, so she decided to go to the kitchen and see if she could help Henry prepare something to eat. If she was hungry, Tate must be ravenous. He seemed to have two hollow legs since his appetite had returned.

"Can I help you, Henry?" Elly asked upon entering the kitchen. "Breakfast was hours ago and I'm hungry. I know Tate will be as hungry as a big bull, too."

"I haven't had time to collect the eggs from the henhouse this morning. I could use some eggs to prepare for the supper meal. I did get one of the men to milk the cows, but they got busy before I could ask him to gather the eggs." Henry explained his situation since he had no kitchen help like he did on the wagon train. "I'll prepare a few sandwiches if you'll collect the eggs."

"I guess I can do that." At least she hoped so. She was a city girl, and her mama had always purchased their eggs at the dry goods store. Elly took the basket hanging on a hook by the door and walked outside. The chicken yard sat about a hundred feet from the back porch. She inched into the yard and shooed a few chickens away from her feet. One big red bird flapped his wings, but it strutted away from her. Good, because he scared her. She continued across the chicken yard, avoiding the chicken droppings scattered over the ground. She opened the henhouse and stepped inside. It was blazing hot, and the smell nearly took her breath away.

Large white, yellow and orange-feathered birds sat on beds of straw. She didn't know how to retrieve the eggs with them sitting and clucking as she moved toward them. "Shoo, birds," she said. "Get off your eggs and let me have them." Elly reached out for one of the white eggs, but withdrew her hand when a hen pecked her finger.

"Ouch," Elly yelled and kissed her hand to stop the flow of blood. "Listen to me. I'm bigger than you are and I want your eggs. Now move and let me have them." The hens continued to cluck and used their beaks as swords to protect their nests.

Elly couldn't go back in the house and say she couldn't get a chicken to move from its nest. Tate would certainly get a good laugh at her expense if she couldn't do something as simple as gathering eggs. With more determination, Elly clapped her hands together to frighten the birds, hoping that the loud sound would make them jump down and leave their roosts.

One enormous hen spread its wings. Suddenly, it flew on top of Elly's head. The hen's claws got caught in her bun. She screamed and twisted her head in all directions, but the big bird got tangled in her hair and dug into her scalp. Elly screamed and tried to cover her head while the chicken pecked her hands. All that clucking and screaming and flapping scared the other hens, and feathers flew in all directions.

Jeremy and Slim came running when they heard her screaming. The chicken yard was in an uproar from the commotion in the henhouse. The rooster was flapping his wings and crowing from the top of his air sacs. Slim warned Jeremy about the bird. "Watch that old rooster. He'll come after you and peck your legs before you can get away."

Slim slung open the henhouse door and was surprised to find Elly sitting on the floor with a big chicken wresting to get loose from her hair. Jeremy rushed in, ripped off his shirt, and covered the bird's head and body. Once the bird calmed down, Slim untangled its claws from Elly's scalp. Blood spattered Elly's face and white feathers were tangled in her hair. Slim wasn't sure if it was Elly's blood or the chicken's.

Once the hen was free, Slim asked if Elly was all right. "Are you hurt anywhere besides the top of your head? Did the old gal peck you in the face or neck?"

Elly held out her hen-pecked hands. "I'm all right. Just weak and near hysteria," She offered a half of a smile. "I've never gathered eggs before, so I figured the chickens would just get up and let me collect them." Slim wanted to laugh, but Elly sounded so pitiful that he didn't dare.

"Normally, we feed the chickens in the yard, and while they

are off their nests, we gather their eggs. Henry should have known better than to send you to do this job so late in the day." Slim walked Elly out of the chicken yard while Jeremy stood guard over the rooster.

"I'm afraid you're going to need a bath, Miss Elly. You have chicken . . . stuff on the back of your dress and other . . . places." He brushed some turds off her shoulder.

"Thank you so much, Slim and you too, Jeremy. I'll go inside and get cleaned up. Oh," she paused and turned to the two men. "Henry said that he needed eggs. Will one of you take care of that for him?"

Once Elly had gone in the house, Slim turned to Jeremy and said, "Henry has no idea that she never lived on a farm or ranch before. One of us had better tell him before he asks her to milk a cow."

Elly removed her dirty dress and underthings. Ugh, it looked like she'd been practically rolling around in chicken poop. It would be a long time before she'd gather eggs again, but she'd insist on some instructions. Those critters were small but protective mothers, and they could do some damage to a person who wanted to take their eggs. Her hands hurt from the puncture holes where the hen had pecked and broken the skin. She donned her old robe and left her bedroom seeking hot water to fill the tub in the water closet.

As soon as she entered the kitchen, she wished she could vanish. Tate munched on a sandwich and regarded her with curious eyes. She stuffed her right hand in the pocket of her robe and placed the other behind her back.

"Good. It looks like Henry has made you a nice lunch. I will eat in a little while, but I want to take a bath right now. Henry," Elly approached the man and said, "May I heat some water for the tub? Do you have a large pail I can use?"

"May I ask why you want to take a bath in the middle of the day? I would think you would rather have a refreshing bath before bed," Tate said, giving her the once-over. "What's wrong with your hand?"

Immediately, Elly regretted reaching for the pail that Henry offered her. "There's nothing wrong with my hand." Elly spun around to go to the pump and fill the pail.

"Stop right there, missy. Show me your hands. I can tell something is wrong with both of them. Why do you have tiny red holes across the top of both hands? Looks like someone took an ice pick to them."

"I'm fine, Mr. Boss Man. Please let me pass so I can get some water to heat for my bath."

Henry turned away from Elly and Tate and began peeling potatoes at a rapid pace. He hummed a little ditty until Tate called his name. "Henry, tell me how this hardhead nurse of mine got these marks on her hands. I know you know something, so start explaining," Tate demanded.

"Leave Henry alone. Can't you see how busy he is?" Elly said.

"Let's hear how you hurt your hands—now. I don't care which one of you tells me, but one of you will."

"It's like this," Elly sighed and began. "I went to the chicken house to gather eggs, and one of the hens jumped on me and pecked my hands while I was trying to get her eggs. Now, are you satisfied? I don't even know how to gather eggs—there, one more stupid thing I did. Go on, laugh if you want to. I know you do."

"Why didn't you tell someone that you didn't know how? You weren't hired to work on the farm. You're here to take care of me, and now look at your hands. You can't hardly care for yourself."

"My hands hurt now, but they'll feel better after a good soaking in soda water," Elly said as she skirted the table where he sat.

"Go back to your bedroom. I will have one of the men bring

you some hot water for your tub bath. You don't need to do anything to cause your hands to bleed more." Tate walked out the screen door and headed toward the barn, yelling, "Jeremy."

In less than thirty minutes, Elly's tub was filled with steamy water. She bathed, then washed her dress and underthings in her wash water. Dressed in a calico blue dress, Elly hung her things in the water closet to drip-dry. Her stomach grumbled, reminding her she hadn't eaten lunch, but first she needed to check Tate's wounds to make sure that they weren't bleeding. Now that they were at his ranch, he'd try to do things that he shouldn't.

Elly found Tate in the office, which was surprising since he was an outdoorsman. He glanced up from his paperwork and gave her a small grin. "How are your hands? Come over here and let me look at them."

Elly slowly entered his office and held out both of her speckled hands, now swelling like small balloons. "You should put salve on them and wrap them in bandages for a few days."

Elly crossed her arms around her chest. "They will be fine just like they are. I can't work if I have bandages on them."

"You aren't here to work," he said roughly. "You're only here to help take care of me, and I am doing fine."

"I need to check your incisions like Doc Weaver told me to. I want to make sure the trip out here didn't cause you to start bleeding again." She bit the inside of her lip. For some reason, being in his home made her nervous.

"All right. Follow me to my room and let's get the examination over with so I can finish my paperwork." He pushed back his desk chair and stalked past her.

"Wait," she called. "Why can't I look at your wounds in the kitchen?"

He turned to her giving her a cocky smile. "Scared to be alone with me, sweetheart?"

When she didn't answer, he continued to his room and stood holding the door for her. He began trying to unbutton his shirt with his right hand. "Here, let me," she said and fidgeted with the buttons. He slipped the shirt off and hung it on the back of his desk chair.

She eased the bandage open and peeked at the exit wound that was now purple and golden in color. The skin had healed inside the large hole, and in a couple of weeks, his shoulder should be back to normal. She circled around to his back and peeled off the smaller bandage. No sign of bleeding. It wasn't going to take as long for the smaller wound to completely heal.

"Well, don't just stand there. How do I look? Can you tell if I'm healing?"

"Yes, both places are looking better. If you don't flex your back and shoulder muscles, the bandages should stay on better, and the bleeding should stop altogether."

"It hurts like hell to go around flexing my muscles, so you don't have to worry your pretty head about me doing that." He reached for his shirt, and she hurried to help him. He stood as still as a statue and seemed to enjoy her buttoning his shirt.

She smiled up at him. "There. I am sure you will be just fine in a week or two. Maybe you can start using your right arm again next week."

Before she knew what he was doing, he pulled her into his arms and kissed her open lips. She should have pushed him back, but she relaxed against his chest and felt her knees almost buckle.

He kissed the side of her neck, her forehead and her closed eyelids. "Please . . . please stop," she whispered in a raspy voice. Careful not to hurt him, she pressed her hands on his chest and lowered her face.

When she raised her head and stepped back, Tate held out a clean white rag for her to tie around his neck as a sling.

Elly sighed. "Tate, you've got to stop . . . manhandling me. I am not your toy." A lump formed in her throat, and tears built up under her eyelids. She should slap his face, but it might hurt him.

He laughed and admitted to himself that he enjoyed her immensely. She was a fighter to the end, even though he knew she enjoyed his advances. "Hurry up and tie the knot in that cloth and help me place it over my head."

Reaching for his right hand, she placed it in the triangle cloth and strode out of his room.

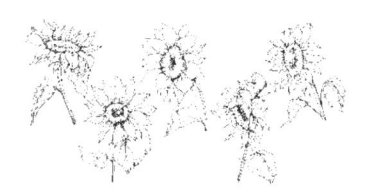

Chapter 21

Early the next morning, Elly helped Henry cook breakfast. He didn't ask her to gather eggs or milk a cow. Tate had warned him about asking her to do anything. After the dishes were washed and put away, Henry said she had to find something else to do. "I don't want to lose this good job. Tate doesn't want you working." Henry took her shoulders and turned her to the outside door.

"I saw some pretty flowers on the fence line when we came here. I think I'll go pick a big bouquet for the dining room table. Do you think that will be all right?" she asked Henry.

"Yes, that would be nice. Picking flowers is not work. Go now and have a nice walk." Henry poured himself a cup of coffee and sat down at the table. Cooking for seven people wasn't like cooking for a wagon train, but it was still demanding because the food was different. Hot biscuits, ham, eggs, pancakes, bacon and sweet rolls were more time-consuming than a huge pot of oatmeal and coffee.

Elly took a pair of scissors out of the desk drawer, headed outside and stood on the back porch. She glanced at the long fence she'd noticed when Major drove them to the ranch. The sun was already high and the morning was warm. Maybe she should have worn one of her bonnets. As she strolled along the brown fence, a big black cow stood all alone in the center of the pasture. She loved the tall sunflowers, but she chose the shorter ones. They were so lovely.

Elly surveyed all the different animals in various fields. Playful ponies romped and kicked up their heels. A few calves were mixed in with the horses, but they stayed close to their mamas. Big white birds sat on the fence posts and watched her walk by. A large group of black crows flew over her head and roosted on the fences further away from her.

Bending down and cutting her fill of sunflowers, she decided to return to the house. Looking back, she didn't realize how far she had walked. She could hardly see the chimney tops on the roofs. Elly wasn't used to walking such a great distant, so she looked at the open field in front of her. A shortcut would take her closer to the ranch house. Crawling through the wood fence, she carried her bundle of flowers and hummed a hymn as she enjoyed the walk and weather. The brown grass was short and a few birds strutted around pecking the fresh piles of manure.

Elly glanced around to see if there were any animals in this field. In the corner a black cow was pawing the ground. Mercy, she thought. I'd better hurry and get on the other side of the fence. Elly was heading for the fence when she heard pounding hooves behind her. The cow was charging toward her. She hiked up her skirt and ran. The faster she raced, the closer it came.

She was looking over her shoulder when she came to a stop. The cow was standing in front of her, pawing the ground and snorting from his nostrils. In trouble again. "Help!" she cried. Again.

The scream echoed all the way to the ranch, and the men who

were working the ponies heard the sound. Another piercing scream and the men jumped on their horses. Jeremy saw Elly first. He leaped over the fence, ripped off his shirt and waved it at the bull.

"Run, Miss. Run to the fence." He hollowed then circled the bull waving his shirt.

Billy, a younger ranch hand, ran to Elly and grabbed her arm. She was staring at the action between Jeremy and the bull. "Come on, woman, hurry!" he cried. He yanked her arm. Finally, she seemed to come out of her daze and followed the young man. He tossed her over the fence. She fell on her butt, but she was safe. Jeremy jumped over the fence and landed on his two feet. He was breathing heavy, his firm body glistening with sweat.

Jeremy stooped to help Elly up on her feet. "Are you all right, Miss?" he asked, worry etched on his face.

"I'm fine, I think. The animal didn't hurt me. Just scared me to death. I didn't know a cow would charge a person."

"Gosh, Miss. He's no cow. Major told us that his young prize bull was still wild. He's out in this field by himself until he can learn to get along with the other animals."

"I saw him earlier, but then I decided to take a shortcut across this field to get to the house quicker," she replied. "I hope you didn't hurt him."

"No, we wouldn't do him any harm. We're just happy that you aren't hurt. Come on and I'll let you ride my horse back to the house."

As Elly stepped toward Jeremy's horse, she nearly fell. Her right hip hurt and gave away as she moved. "You are hurt," Jeremy declared. "Tate will kill us."

"Tate? Why would he do you harm because I got hurt. You didn't do anything to me."

"We were told not to allow you to work or get hurt while

you're here, you being a city gal and all."

"Oh, my goodness. We just won't tell him anything. Promise me you'll keep this quiet. He doesn't have to know—"

Jeremy sucked in his breath and nodded at her. Elly knew in an instant. "He's standing behind me . . . right?" Jeremy slowly bobbed his head up and down. The blood drained out of her face. This man was going to kill her if his prize bull was harmed in any way.

"Get on back to the ranch house, boys. I'll take care of my nurse." Tate said softly, which surprised Elly.

Squaring her shoulders, she twisted around and nearly fell because of the pain that shot through her backside. Blood showed through his shirt. At the same time, she saw his horse wandering around near the fence.

"Oh, just look at your chest. You're bleeding again." She reached to touch his chest, but he took her hand in his.

"Elly, are you all right?" He asked softly. "I can tell you have hurt your butt or hip. You know you need a protector when you leave the house. One of these days you're going to harm yourself."

Elly stepped back from his hold on her, lifted her chin and glared at him. "I'm not a child, Tate. I don't need a guardian to watch over me. Things . . . things just happen. I don't go outside looking for trouble."

Tate stared at her like she was a little tiger who had pulled out her claws. "I didn't mean that you're a child. I wouldn't want to kiss a little girl." He smiled at the rosy blush seeping over her cheeks. "When I heard your screams, my heart stopped beating. I thought you were in the kitchen with Henry."

"I was for a while." She omitted that she had helped Henry clean the kitchen. "I decided to go for a walk and pick some wildflowers for the dining-room table." She limped to the fence and nodded to the open field. "I was going to take a shortcut back to the house. I didn't see the small black cow . . . bull, I mean. He charged so fast I didn't know what to do." Her head hung down. "I didn't mean to scare you or the men, but I'm thankful Jeremy heard me."

"How did you manage to hurt yourself?" He asked.

"Billy tossed me over the fence and I landed on my backside, and then he leaped over to safety."

"Come on, let's get back to the house and have a look at that hip. You could have broken it."

"No, I mean it's not broken. I wouldn't be able to walk if it was broke. I just need to soak in a hot tub and I'll be fine. We need to look at your wound. You must have hurt yourself riding your horse. You know the doctor hasn't given your permission to ride yet."

"Woman, your screams made my hair stand up straight. Do you think I was going to walk this far from the house and see what mischief you had gotten into?"

"Stop calling me *Woman*. It sounds so ugly." Elly strode to his horse. "You ride and I'll walk beside you to the house."

"Woman, you have lost your mind. Climb up on the fence if you can, and I will help you onto the saddle. You don't need to be walking on your hip. Don't give me any sass or I just might—" he sighed. "Just do as I say."

Pleased he didn't come out to the pasture to scold her about how stupid she was, and also pleased he didn't say that a child would have known better than to climb in a field with a bull, she obeyed his command. Climbing up on the fence with his help, she wriggled to get comfortable on the horse's saddle. She was afraid of the horse, but her hip hurt too bad to walk.

As they headed back to the house, Doc Weaver's black carriage was parked near the back door. "I never thought I'd be glad to see that old man, but his timing is perfect. He can look at your hip." His eyes locked with hers. "Don't even think about objecting, young lady, unless you want me to help him undress you and hold you down."

"You're a mean brute, you know that?" Elly looked down at

the sunflowers next to the fence. "I dropped my flowers, and they were so pretty," she said, her lip protruding.

"We'll pick some more later." Tate said as he led the horse up to the back porch.

After Doctor Weaver gave Elly a thorough exam, he told her that she would be fine in a few days. "Your hip isn't broken, but you'll have a big bruise on your backside, and it will hurt to sit. Use a pillow for comfort and lie on your stomach when you sleep." He snapped his bag closed.

"Thank you, doctor. I feel so much better knowing that I'm only bruised. I'm thankful that I didn't land on my head when Billy tossed me over the fence." She giggled.

Tate was standing in the doorway of her bedroom. "I'm thankful that my bull didn't gore you in the back while you were running around screaming."

"I wasn't running until Jeremy came to my rescue. I guess I scared the little bull when I showed up. He was pawing the ground and snorting when he saw me." Elly limped past Tate and stopped in the doorway.

"Doctor Weaver, would you like a cup of coffee after you check Tate over. The front of his shirt has blood on it. I believe he opened the wound when he rode his horse."

"You rode your horse after I told you not to?" Doc Weaver whirled around and shouted at Tate. Elly smiled to herself and continued to the kitchen.

"I had no choice," he mumbled as he watched the little tattletale priss from the room. If she didn't already have a hurt hip, he'd enjoy turning her over his knee and blistering her sassy butt.

Tate's wound had bled a little, but not enough for the doctor to be too upset. He followed Tate into the kitchen and straddled a chair. "Black coffee for me, little gal," he called to Elly.

"Would you like a cup too, Mr. Maynard? Cream and sugar?"

"After weeks on the trail, you know how I like my coffee."

"Oh, yes, I remember now. Would you both like a leftover biscuit with some cold ham? Henry has a few left from breakfast."

"No, but I understand from Mrs. Duffy that you bake pies. I shore would like to have a piece next time I'm out here."

"Miss Eddy will only be here for a week, remember?" Tate peered at the old doctor. "Maybe you can get some of her pies at the rooming house," Tate replied.

"Well, I'd better get on over to the Jemison's' place. Mrs. Jemison's time is getting close and I told her husband I would come by and check on her." He pushed his chair back and stood. "Stay off your horse, young man, and you, gal, get off that hip and rest."

Chapter 22

The next morning, Elly was surprised that her hip and butt still hurt. She had a restless night so she excused herself and went and lay down on her bed. Her nerves were shaken and her hip hurt with every move. As she got comfortable on top of the covers, she drifted off to sleep. *She ran from a big black bull as he chased her through a field of sunflowers.* She tossed and turned, feeling pain all through her body, but she had to get away from that wild animal. "*Stay away from my flowers, you big brute,*" she mumbled in her sleep.

Tate was walking from his room when he heard Elly talking in her bedroom. Who was in her room with her? He jerked open her door. Surprised, he saw her all tangled up in her bedcovers and wrestling with a pillow that laid on her chest.

"Go away, go away. You're ruining my sunflowers," she said, her eyes closed and her face covered with sweat.

Tate stood over the bed watching her writhe in pain. Tears dripped onto the sheet and she cried out in pain. "Oh, my hip is broken. Boss man is going to kill me."

Boss Man, I can't believe she calls me that ugly name. Elly thinks I would do her harm. He rubbed his hand over the wound on his chest. *I would never hurt a hair on her head.*

"Elly, Elly," he called to her. "Wake up, sweetheart. You're having a bad dream." He gently touched the arm that was hugging her pillow. She moaned and continued to cry out in her sleep while trying to get comfortable, then rolled over. Her skirt had rolled up to her waist, He studied her body for a minute. How bad was she hurt? Slowly he reached for the waistband of her bloomers and pulled them away from her skin. He peeked down past her waist to see her backside.

"What are you doing?" Elly rolled over and sat straight up in bed, then cried out from the pain.

Tate jumped back from the edge of the bed. Before he could explain his actions, Elly spoke loudly, "I can't believe you were attempting to see my . . . private parts! What kind of man are you? Are you one of those nasty old men who attack young women while they sleep?"

"Shut your stupid mouth, woman. You know better than that. You were crying in your sleep, and I just wanted to see how bad you were hurt. I am not some old man that would ever do you harm, and you know it." Tate snorted like the little bull in the pasture.

Elly giggled and covered her mouth with the pillow. Tate was standing over her with a crimson face and clenched fists. She had never seen him so embarrassed.

"What's so damn funny?"

"You are," she said losing control of her laughter. "Standing over me . . . trying to peek . . . at my backside like a sleazy peeping tom. I would have never thought in a million years you would do something like that."

"Oh, you," Tate said, his face getting redder. "I wanted to help you, not leap on your hurt body while you were sleeping. I know your backside is hurting you something awful. Get out of bed and put on your nightclothes. I'm going to make you a drink that will help you rest, and no, it won't be the medicine the doctor gave me."

In a few minutes, Tate knocked on her bedroom door. He was carrying a small glass. She slowly shifted to her side.

"Sit up for a minute. Take it easy. Now drink this and you'll feel better soon."

"What is this?" She moved the glass under her nose. "It smells like whiskey." Not giving Tate a chance to answer, she continued. "I don't drink alcohol, Buster. You can keep your foul-smelling drink." She pushed the glass back.

"No, missy, you will drink this if I have to pour it down your throat myself. You tortured me with a drink when I first got shot—now it's my turn to get revenge." He smiled. "Drink." Tate stood above her holding the glass of medicine, as he called it. "I'm waiting."

Realizing she had no choice, she reached for the golden-brown liquid and downed it in a single swallow. Her throat burned as she struggled to breathe. She fought to keep the medicine down. Her eyes filled with tears and mumbled an unladylike phrase. "You have a vindictive streak in you, Mr. Maynard."

Tate tossed his head back and laughed. "Good girl," he said and turned to leave the room. "Rest now and I will see you at supper." He closed the door as she lay back down on her side.

Later, when the men gathered for lunch, Major asked Tate about Elly. "Is she having lunch in her room?"

"I looked in on her before I came in the kitchen and she's still sleeping. She really took a fall on her backside when she was tossed over the fence." Tate glanced at Billy whose face reddened.

"I didn't mean to hurt her, really I didn't," he said.

"We all know that," Tate replied. "She had a bad night and didn't rest very well, so I gave her a couple large shots of whiskey in some water to help her relax."

"Gracious, son. Were you trying to knock her out for a couple of days? A person as small as she is, and not used to drinking, could be out for a while."

"If she isn't up by supper, I'll wake her." Tate said a little sheepishly. "She was crying out in her sleep. I just wanted to help her rest."

"I'm sure she'll be fine when she does wake up. I suggest you give her some work in the house to keep her busy when she isn't looking after you. You can find something in the office for her to do." Major walked over to the hat rack and retrieved his Stetson. "The fellows are going to brand the new cows that arrived early this morning. We'll be next to the barn if you want to come watch." He pushed open the screen door and called to the men who were still enjoying their lunch. "Hurry on out, boys. We got a lot more work to do today."

Tate sat at the kitchen table with Henry. "I'm so sick of being laid up. If I could get my hands on Bill Sawyer, I'd strangle him for shooting me." Tate stood and carried his fresh coffee to his office.

At supper time, Henry missed Elly's company and help. Tate had said she didn't need to be working in the hot kitchen. If she wanted to make a pie or two, that would be fine, but she wasn't his kitchen helper. If Henry needed help, Tate said he would hire someone from town.

After Henry rang the supper bell and Elly had not appeared, Tate knocked on her door. When she didn't answer, he peeked in her room. She was still under the covers snoring softly. Tate closed the door and allowed her to continue to rest. He shouldn't have made her drink so much whiskey.

Tate told the men that Elly was fine but just resting. She would be with them at breakfast. He hoped she would wake up on her own, but if not, he'd have to sober her up. He grinned at the hangover she was probably going to have. She'd lay into him for getting her drunk.

By suppertime the next day, Elly was sitting on the side of her bed, holding her head. Why did her head ache so much? Every footstep in the house sounded like someone was pounding on the floor.

Tate knocked on her door and she whispered, "Come in."

"Why are you whispering?"

"Why are you screaming?" she replied while holding her head.

"Here, I have a special powder for you to take. This is good stuff, and it will help the pain between your eyes go away."

"How did you know I would need this?" When he didn't answer, she asked. "How long have I been asleep?"

He marched over to her window, pulled the curtains back and pushed the window open. Then he turned to face her. "Maybe a day and a half. Possibly two days?"

"How much of the foul stuff did you give me to drink? It was nearly straight whiskey. You got me drunk, didn't you?" She raised her voice, but regretted it immediately. "Oh, my head."

"Here, now drink up and I promise you'll feel like new in a little while."

"You said something like that before . . . you snake in the grass."

He laughed and watched her swallow the powder. He offered her a water chaser, but she asked, "What's in this water?"

"You are too much, Miss Eddy. You don't have a trusting bone in your body. Please get dressed and come to supper. My men think I may have harmed you in some way for scaring my little bull half to death."

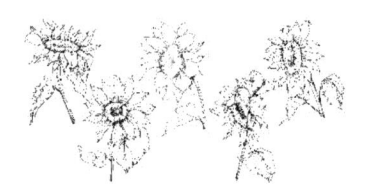

Chapter 23

All the men jumped up from the table when Elly entered the dining room. After formalities, she took her seat next to Major.

"So good to see you awake and moving around so much better. I hope your injury is nearly well." Major said while passing a big bowl of boiled potatoes.

"Yes, I am much better, thank you. I'm not ready to go for another long walk yet." She smiled at the men. "But I can sit without pain. Now that I'm on the mend, I'll make pies for my rescuers."

The men cheered and began putting in their favorite pie request. Elly laughed at their enthusiasm. Her head didn't pain her nearly as bad as it did when she first woke up. She even managed a smile for Tate.

"Miss Elly, Tate has work in the office that you can assist him with, if you don't mind. We'd like for you to help in the office when you're not attending him. There's some correspondence and other pieces of mail that could use attention."

"Certainly, Major. I'll be glad to do whatever Tate wishes for me to do. I can start first thing in the morning, if that is okay for you."

Early the next morning after breakfast, Elly prepared two

different types of pies for the men to enjoy at lunch and supper. She baked two apple and two peach pies. She wasn't sure what Tate's favorite was, but she would soon find out. After she straightened the kitchen, she went in search of Tate and his office.

The house had a curious stillness about it. Some ashes fell from a log in the parlor fireplace, but other than that, birds sang near the open windows. Tate must be in the house. After breakfast, she didn't notice that he'd gone outside. She slowly pushed open the door to the office. He was stretched out on the soft brown couch with a book in his left hand while his right arm lay on his chest in the sling.

Once he sensed someone in the room, he rose and told her to come inside. "You finished baking the pies. I can smell them in here. I know the men will be happy to have a special dessert for lunch."

"Yes, I'm ready to help you with the paperwork that Major mentioned."

After about a half hour of instructions, he excused himself and left her alone to answer some letters, requests, and pay a few invoices. It felt good to go outside and do a few odd jobs around the ranch. He was tired of feeling helpless.

Tate wasn't a man to pour out his feelings. But with Elly around, he felt content and comfortable. He had always felt he needed to be doing something, to be on the move. Being in one place was never something he wanted. But after selling the wagons and settling in at the ranch, it felt right. Elly made it feel special. He enjoyed sitting at his desk while she organized the mail into stacks. The little twist of her mouth as she read some of the correspondence made him smile. Yes, he was happy for the first time in years, but he wanted more—whatever that was. He wasn't sure, but something in his life was missing.

After supper Elly sat in the swing on the front porch and listened to one of the men play his guitar and sing a country ballad. The young man had a good voice and Tate said that he sang occasionally in church. It had been a long day, so Elly went to the water closet and dressed for bed.

Early the next morning, Elly enjoyed sitting on the back porch before everyone stirred. She enjoyed the sounds of the farm animals and loved watching the sunrise. The beautiful shades of gold and purple were the most beautiful portraits she'd ever seen.

The last thing she remembered was the sun peeking above the horizon. Then something hit her in the back of the head.

After Elly opened her eyes, her head ached as she reached for the back of her skull. She felt something sticky and wet as she rubbed her hair—blood? Something or someone had hit her hard with something sharp. Glancing around the strange room, she dragged herself off the floor and stood on wobbly legs. Her vision blurred, but as she surveyed her surroundings, Elly realized it was a shack. It appeared that it might fall down if a good wind came. The sound of wood being chopped made her head pound. All she wanted to do was lie down on the floor and sink into a blissful sleep.

With a loud thump, a brown feedbag was tossed at her feet. She jumped back against the wall and stared into the eyes of Bill Sawyer. He'd come into the one-room shack without her noticing him. That was scary. The hit on the head must have done more damage to her than she thought.

"How did I get here? The last thing I remember I was on the back porch."

"Yep, you made a mighty fine sight sitting in that swing staring out over the horizon. I hated to have to hit you, but it couldn't be helped. I needed you to be unconscious, so you wouldn't scream and wake the others."

"What do you want with me? I have nothing of value, and I certainly will never be your bride."

"I don't want a bride, but if I did, you would be a great replacement. I could make you marry me, if that's what I wanted from you." He grinned at her, making her skin scrawl.

"I need money and your boyfriend has plenty. He will pay handsomely for your safe return."

"You are mistaken. I don't have a boyfriend who'd be willing to pay to get me away from you."

"I ain't no fool, lady, and I shore ain't blind. Everyone in town knows you're Maynard's woman." He gave her a look that dared her to dispute his statement. "I'll put more wood into the fireplace while you open those cans and fix us something to eat. Be careful, woman. I don't want to kill you before I get my ransom."

Elly stood paralyzed with fear. A sickly dread went through her body at the thought of never seeing Tate again. And her baby brother, Timmy. She clutched her stomach as she attempted to pick up the bag of canned goods. As she swayed, she moved slowly to the wooden table. Gripping the edge, Elly picked up a sharp knife and looked at it. This could be a weapon, she thought.

"Go ahead, honey. Try to kill me with that blade. Nothing I'd like better than slapping a pretty gal around," her captor said, as he drank from a jug that contained rye whiskey.

Elly made it to the table and poured the beans into a small pot that sat in the center. She didn't care if it was clean or not; she wouldn't be eating any of it. She walked on unsteady legs over to the fireplace and hung the pot over the fire. Her head pounded with every step she took. She was thankful that her head wasn't bleeding anymore.

"Slice that loaf of fresh bread, too," he demanded as he sipped on the whiskey.

Elly removed the hot beans from the fire and sliced the bread. She found several tin plates on a shelf and poured the food into one, setting it at the end of the table. Moving away, Elly watched the burly man eat and sip from the jug. He burped and laughed like an ill-mannered fool.

"I need to go to the outhouse--please," Elly said. She prayed this shack had a place where a person could have some privacy, but that was not to be.

He grabbed her arm and pushed her toward the open front door. "Look out there, Beautiful. There's your outhouse. Pick any tree, but I'll be watching. Don't try to run away from me."

Elly shook loose from his hold and walked away from him. The cool fresh air felt so good. She chose a huge oak tree and relieved herself. The sound of the crickets and birds made her head hurt, but she wanted to linger outside. She gazed into the dark sky and prayed that awful man would pass out from the liquor. The thought that he might want to try to have his way with her scared her to death. "Please Lord, please, please give me the courage to handle my situation. I know Tate and his men will be searching for me."

"Come over here, woman," Bill Sawyer said and tossed a blanket near the fireplace. Elly inched toward him. "Hold out your hands," he said and hiccupped. "Pardon me, madam," he slurred and grinned like an idiot. "You'll sleep tied to me, so you won't get any ideas about trying to leave during the night."

He gave her a shove and she stumbled onto the blanket. The fool had gotten drunk, so she didn't want to do anything to upset him. She had learned that much from living with her own drunken papa. "Don't say or do anything to rile your pa," her mama would warn her and Timmy.

In the darkness she had no idea where she was. Escaping tonight wasn't an option. Suddenly, he grabbed her wrist and wrapped the rope around it and around his wrist. His head didn't hit the floor before he was snoring. He had drunk nearly the whole bottle of whiskey. "Thank you, Lord," Elly murmured.

Early the next morning, the brute had cut her ropes and she lay on the blanket alone—thank the Lord. She heard him stomping around outside, so she stood and straightened her dress and pushed her hair out of her eyes. A field mouse skirted in front of the fireplace giving her a fright.

In a few minutes, Bill Sawyer charged into the shack with a piece of paper and a pencil. "Sit over here and write what I say to your lover boy. I'm asking money for your return and I want to tell him where to make the drop."

"If you want money for me, you write the note," Elly said, acting braver than she really was.

"Shut your mouth and write what I say, and be quick about it," he demanded as he pulled out a chair for her to sit at the table. "Don't give me no sass, woman."

This was one mean man, and he could and would hurt her for the least little cause. Using a much nicer tone of voice, she asked him, "What do you want me to say?"

"Tell him I want five thousand dollars in small bills delivered to my farm and place the money bag in the well bucket. Sign my name."

Elly wrote his first name on the paper. Is this how you spell your name? She held the paper out to him.

"Yep, that's my name." he said. "Write what I say, woman, or I may have to mess up your pretty face."

Elly realized that this man couldn't read because she wrote his name as *I'm scared to death, Help!*

Bill Sawyer demands $5,000.00 for my return from the north pasture in a line shack not too far from town. Place the money at his farm beside the well in a bucket. Please hurry.

"Here," Elly said, "you want to read it?"

"No, you read back to me what you wrote, and you'd better not have written anything else."

Elly gave him an exasperated look and read, "Whom It May Concern. I have your woman, Elly. I want $5,000.00 for her safe return. Bring small bills to my farm and place the money at the well in a big bucket today before three o'clock."

"Well, that's mighty fine. I couldn't have done any better myself. Cook some coffee, sausage and bread, and I'll be on my way to deliver this note. I will have to tie you so you need to eat and go out again like you did last night. After the drop, I'll tell somebody where they can find you."

Elly sat in the straight-backed chair at the table with her hands and feet tied. She listened to Bill Sawyer ride away. "Thank you, Lord. I do feel sorry for this man, but I pray he's caught before he harms someone else. I hope I gave Tate enough information to find me before he returns. Amen."

Once Elly was sure that Bill Sawyer had ridden away from the line shack, she struggled to get her feet and hands untied. She sat on the edge of the chair and used one foot to push down on top of the ropes tied around her ankles. She wiggled and wiggled her feet while stretching and pulling on the thin rope. Giving her feet a rest, she bit down on the rope that had her wrists tied. Almost immediately the rope slipped from the tight knot, giving her hope that she could untie herself. She continued to bite and pull the rope with her teeth until the first knot was loose. It took forever, but she freed her hands from the ropes. Afterward, it was easy to loosen the ties around her feet.

Elly limped to the door and peeked out. Hurrying outside to the big tree by the back door, she relieved herself. Once her personal needs were taken care of, she went back into the shack to see if she could find anything to help her survive in the woods. A blanket would help and the small tin on the mantle held matches. She tucked the tin in her pocket and tossed the blanket over her shoulder.

But in what direction should she go? The fool had brought her here on horseback, but she was nearly unconscious. She had no idea which direction would take her to town or to Tate's ranch. Deciding that it didn't matter, she just had to stay hidden in the woods until she recognized the search party.

Feeling a bit braver, she stuck to the edge of the main trail for hours. The sun had come out making her hot. This was fall, but it still felt like summer during the middle hours of the day. She had walked until the sun started to set when she saw an abandoned cave in a thicket of trees.

Fashioning a torch with a few sticks, she held it up to see inside. Drops of water spilled down the side of the cave forming a pool. She didn't see any ground critters or grizzly bears, so she gathered more wood and built a bonfire in front of the cave's entrance. She gathered several large bushes and brushed off an area for her to place the blanket on the ground. After making another trip outside for her personal needs, she gathered more firewood. Elly felt safe for the first time today.

Chapter 24

Tate scowled. How dumb he was not to think that Bill Sawyer wouldn't return to the area. Since the man owned a farm, he should have known he might come back and get some of his things. The sheriff had assured him Bill had left Sunflower and the marshals in other counties would catch him. He should have realized the foolish man felt rejected and was embarrassed in front of the whole town. A man like Bill Sawyer would hold a grudge even if he'd brought the situation on himself.

Sensing his uneasiness, Tate's horse pawed the ground. "All right, boy, we're going. The sheriff and his men will be here soon," he said and patted the animal's neck. Tate lifted his face to feel the full impact of the cool breeze. His back hurt as he tried to sit tall in the saddle. The old doctor had told him not to ride for another two weeks because he may open up his wound on his shoulder and back. His shoulder pained like someone was stabbing him with a knife, but he couldn't give in to the pain.

"Let's ride," Sheriff Murray yelled to the posse. Sheriff Murray had sworn in about a dozen men who could be away from their farms for a day or two, but not much longer. After a long warm day of searching caves and abandoned shacks, questioning people and searching for fresh horse prints, they camped near the river.

Tate's shoulder hurt like it was on fire, but he didn't complain. While the men were sympathetic to his situation, they were not nursemaids or endearing like a woman would be.

Sheriff Murray passed Tate a hot cup of coffee and a piece of hardtack. "Well, son, we've searched everywhere in this county for two days. Our only hope is that fool will send a ransom note. Surely he didn't kidnap Miss Eddy for himself. He needs money to get out of the territory. In the morning we'll head back to town, so the men can go home to their families. Then we'll wait to hear from Bill."

Tate asked one of the younger men if he would assist him with unsaddling his horse for the night, and he was happy to help him. "I'll saddle him for you in the morning too, Mr. Maynard," he said.

"Thanks, Jimmy." He tossed him a silver dollar.

"Wow, sir, you don't have to pay me, but I sure can use the money. Thanks again."

Early the next morning, after the fire was put out and the coffeepot cleaned, Tate spoke to Sheriff Murray. "I'm not going back with you. I'm going to continue searching on my own today. I'll send you word when I'm back at my ranch."

"If you're sure, boy. Be careful with that arm. Your pa's probably gonna be mad as dickens, but you already know that. See you soon."

Tate watched as the men headed toward town. He walked his horse to the edge of the river and allowed him to drink. Pulling himself onto his horse, he nearly screamed from the excruciating agony caused from his wounds. He couldn't give in to the suffering he was enduring while Elly was still missing and possibly hurt bad, too. He had to find her. His heart felt like it had been torn out of his chest when he was told that she had disappeared while sitting on the back porch. After searching the house and outside, blood was discovered on the ground. A few pieces of clothing were lying on the path to the clotheslines. With fresh horse prints, they had agreed a man must have taken her. A man—but who had done this to Elly—his Elly, if not Bill Sawyer?

Tate couldn't keep his mind on the ground that he was supposed to be searching. His thoughts were all about finding Elly safe. From the first time he laid eyes on the dark-haired beauty, he felt like his guts were torn upside down. He loved the way she nursed him back to health, determined to save his arm. Irritable and bored, he was a terrible patient but she never left him. She was a worthy adversary whom he enjoyed baiting. There was never a dull moment spent with her.

With the sun going down behind the trees and hills, riding had taken a toll on his sore body. He needed a stiff drink for sure to help relieve the pain. He walked slowly up a ridge and stopped his horse and surveyed his surroundings. There was an old mining cave close by. Maybe if he could find it, he'd spend the night inside. He didn't want to camp out in the cold air.

As he sat in his saddle, looking around, he caught a glimpse of movement behind a tree right in front of him. Could that be an animal? No, he thought, it wasn't an animal because it would be trying to climb the tree. He eased his horse a little closer. A piece of material sat near the root of the tree, and before he called out, there was another movement. "Who's there?"

Elly had heard a horse and rider come up the hillside. She'd been outside gathering firewood, praying that the sheriff or Tate would have gotten the ransom note and was now out searching for her. She pressed her body against the tree trunk and waited to get a good look at whoever was riding near. She held her breath and tucked her skirt behind the tree because the rider was approaching her hiding place.

"Elly," Tate said softly at first. Then he called her name louder. "Elly, Elly."

She let out her breath and peeked around the tree to see her Boss Man sitting on his big horse shading his eyes from the glare of the sunset. She grabbed the hem of her dirty skirt, screamed his name and ran toward him.

"Tate, oh Tate, here I am, It's me," she called as she came stumbling from behind the big tree. Before he could get down, Elly's screaming and waving her hands in the air scared his horse, and the steed sidestepped a few feet and attempted to rear his front hoofs. Tate was trying to get his horse under control, but his face was full of pain.

Elly reached for Tate. She grabbed onto his shirtfront, causing him to lose his balance. His tall frame slid out of the saddle, hitting the hard ground.

"Oh damn," he shrieked and rolled over on his good side. Elly knelt down beside him. She lifted his head and shoulders trying to make him more comfortable. "Oh, I'm so sorry."

"Elly," he moaned, "I think you've managed . . . to kill . . . me this time." He fainted in her arms.

"Tate, Tate, please wake up." Blood. She immediately tore the shirtfront open and saw that several stitches had busted loose, and blood was staining his bandage. She laid him down on the ground, reached for the canteen tied to the saddle horn, and encouraged him to drink. Water rolled off his lips without swallowing. She wet her hands and patted his face. He didn't even blink.

Elly glanced around the area for anything, anyone. The sunset began setting behind the hillside. It was almost dark and the air was much cooler. She had to get Tate into her hideout before it was too dark for her to see.

Elly had spent her first night away from the shack in the old miners' cave. With no idea how to get back to town or Tate's ranch, she was afraid to get too far away from her hideout in case Bill Sawyer tracked her and found her on the trail. She planned to wait for the sheriff's men to come in search of her.

She had to get Tate up on his feet and walk him over to the

cave. She patted his face with water, but it didn't help to wake him. She turned the canteen over and covered his face with water. He shook his head and started coughing.

"Tate, please help me get you to the cave. You must stand so I can help you walk. Please sit up." Tate never said a word, but he let her help him stand. "Hold tight to the saddle horn with your good arm."

Tate leaned into his horse and dragged his boots. He wasn't fully awake but conscious enough to follow instructions. Holding him on the other side, they managed to get to the entrance of the cave. Elly guided him to a clean area near the fire and settled him on the ground. He passed out again.

Elly led his horse inside the cave and untied Tate's bedroll. She spread one blanket over his tall body and folded the other to make a pillow upon which to lay his head. Then she watched him sleep. Her backside still ached, but she had no time to think about herself. Standing up, she hurried outside and gathered the wood she'd left near the tree. Looking up at the stars, she said a prayer. "Thank you, Jesus. Thank you for leading Tate to me. Please don't let him die. I love him with all my heart."

Inside the cave, she made a fire which gave off enough light to see the interior. In the back of the cave was a small stream that flowed down the rock wall from outside somewhere. The water was crystal clear and refreshing. She led Tate's horse to the stream and loosened up his saddle and removed the bit from his mouth. She didn't remove the saddle because she wasn't strong enough to put it back on by herself. On the trail, one of the men always tossed it over on the horses' back for her. Sometimes she stood on a large box.

After making sure Tate was still breathing, she walked outside and pulled up an armful of tall grass to feed the horse. Once she fed him, she searched through Tate's saddlebags to see if he had something she could eat. She had survived on dried-up blackberries.

In one saddlebag, Tate had a can of beans, coffee, and hardtack. In the other one was a small boiler, a coffee pot, a cup, plate, two spoons and a clean rag with a bar of soap. She was thankful that cowboys were always prepared on the open range.

After building the fire back up, she warmed the beans while the coffee was boiling. Food never tasted so good. She saved some beans just in case Tate woke up.

Elly washed Tate's face several times with a cool rag and the bar of soap she had found in his saddlebag. He was dead to the world, but she couldn't find any kind of knot on his head. She had no idea what caused him to be unconscious, other than the pain. She hated that she was so excited to see him that she caused him to fall off his horse and land on his wounds. Everything she did around him ended in some type of disaster. The school superintendent in Leesville had called her a jinx. May she was one after all.

Elly sat cross-legged in front of Tate. Tears washed down her cheeks. All night she watched him sleep. She wiped his face over and over and tried to make him drink water. He had to wake up. Maybe the fall from his horse broke a rib that could have punctured his lungs. She thought of all kinds of things that could cause him to be unconscious.

Finally near daybreak, Tate opened his eyes and pulled her close to his body. She snuggled against him, his muscled arms enclosed around her. She was careful not to hurt his bad shoulder. "I love you, Tate," she whispered softy. Her words brought a quickening to his loins and peace to his mind. He fell back to sleep with her wrapped in his arms.

Voices came from outside the cave, but Elly thought it was all a dream. She had been so tired that the earth could have moved before it disturbed her.

Tate was in so much pain that he had awakened but didn't want to move without Elly's help. He continued to snuggle up against her and placed small kisses on her neck. She groaned and smiled in her sleep.

Tate's horse had wandered out and stood at the entrance eating the tall grass as the sheriff's posse rode by and spotted the animal. One of the men jumped down off his horse and entered the cave. He came out laughing. "They're in the cave all lovey-dovey like. I thought they disliked each other."

Another man's loud boastful voice disturbed the peace and quiet in the cave. "Sheriff, come see our two missing people all wrapped up in each other's arms. I guess this is a new way to protect our women folks," he said, slapping his hand on his leg as he walked out of the cave.

The sheriff hopped down from his horse and entered the cave. Elly was awake and sitting up beside Tate. "Well, I'm glad to see you both alive."

"Oh, Sheriff, I am so happy to see you. Listen, Tate is hurt badly again. He fell off his horse and tore some of his stitches loose. We need a stretcher or a wagon to carry him back to town. He cannot sit and ride a horse." Elly stood, taking the sheriff's hand in her own. "Please, help him."

"I can ride, Sheriff," Tate said in a matter-of-fact tone.

"No, he cannot. Don't listen to him. His wounds have bled all night and he needs Doc Weaver to care for him as soon as possible. I have been treating his wounds for him. He's in awful pain."

"Lie still, Tate, while I get the men to build a travois to pull you home. It won't be a comfortable ride, but it's better than having to wait for a wagon from town."

"There's no need. I said I can ride. Pay that woman no attention."

"Do I need to hogtie you, son? I can see traces of blood all over your shirt and pants. I am not going to allow you to ride your horse, and a travois will be quicker."

Once the sheriff left the cave, Elly turned her temper on Tate. "Now, I'm back to being *that woman* again? Thanks for telling the sheriff that I'm a dumb, histrionic female who doesn't know what she is talking about. A woman who nearly killed you. Well, mister, when we get back home, you'll need to find yourself another gal to paw and kiss when you feel like it." She spun around and stormed out of the cave.

After the men cut down two slim trees and made long poles out of them, they looped them together with ropes and placed two blankets over the ropes to form a mattress. Soon, they were ready to travel with Tate's long frame positioned behind his horse. The men snickered about being careful with the soon-to-be groom. The sheriff gave the men a dirty look, which only made them laugh more.

Chapter 25

Old Doc Weaver declared Tate to be in a bad way. "Son, you ain't never going to get well. I'll probably have to amputate your arm before you allow it to get better. Stitches torn loose can only cause infection. It's a good thing you have an attentive nurse who's willing to sit and watch over you night and day. I mean it, Tate. If you bust open your wound on this shoulder again, I don't know if I can save your arm." He snapped his old bag closed and handed Major a bottle of medicine. "His nurse knows what to do with this stuff. I'll be back in a day or two."

Major walked the doctor to the door and gave him a few dollars. "Thanks for coming out so soon, doc."

"I don't mind riding out here. You folks are the only people who pay me in cash." He shoved the money in his pocket, plopped down into his rickety carriage and drove away.

Elly was in the water closet taking a long hot bath when Major returned to Tate's room to give him some medicine. The patient was lying on his back with his good arm covering his eyes. He looked miserable.

Major stood at the side of Tate's bed. He poured a spoon of medicine and told Tate to open up and swallow. Tate glared at him, but did as he was told. He complained about how the medicine made him feel after he woke up, but he needed something to help relieve the pain.

"Son, I'm curious. How did you manage to fall off your horse? I can't remember a time since you were little that you did such a thing."

"I didn't fall," he exploded. Shifting to get comfortable, he said, "Elly pulled me off. She was so happy to see me she came running out from behind a tree, waving and screaming. Scared my horse. He tried to rear up when she grabbed my shirt and pulled me off. I landed on my bad shoulder. The pain was so bad I lost consciousness."

"One more thing before Miss Elly comes back in to see you," Major whispered, then walked to the door and glanced down the hall. "What's this talk about you and her getting married? When did you ask her?"

"I haven't asked her to marry me," he growled. "Those fools came in the cave and we were asleep . . . in a compromised position. I was holding her in my arms because we were cold. Nothing happened, for gosh sakes. I could hardly move, much less fool around with a woman."

"I see," said his pa. "Has Miss Elly heard any of this gossip?"

"I'm not sure, but the men were laughing and talking among themselves. They made sure I heard them." His words slurred, then he closed his eyes. He was in a better world for a few hours.

Major was opening Tate's window to bring in fresh air when Elly came in the room.

"Major, did the doctor leave medicine for Tate?"

"Yes, he did. I gave him a dose and it worked fast. He's already asleep, but he was in a lot of pain."

"Yes, he was and will be for a while, again. I'm so sorry. His wounds were almost healed, but I caused him to fall off the horse and reopen his stitches." She lowered her face to hide her tears.

"Elly," Major took her and cradled her in his big arms. "Tate knows you didn't intend for him to fall off his horse. He told me that, and he was so happy to find you safe."

"Oh Major, your son may not blame me, but he doesn't want me around any longer."

"Did he say that to you?"

"Well, not in those words, but he said that I had almost managed to kill him when he fell to the ground before he passed out." She whirled and ran from the room. Tears flowed freely from her eyes as she packed her small carpetbag. She had already asked Slim to drive her back to town.

Major was standing on the front porch. When Slim drove the wagon to the front of the house, he helped her into the wagon. "Elly, Tate needs you. Please reconsider and stay."

"I can't." She wiped tears from her cheeks. "Please hire another nurse for him. He'll need help bathing, getting dressed, and having his bandages changed."

"He's going to be upset with you for leaving."

"No, he won't. He'll be relieved that this dumb woman is out of his life. Good-bye, Major, and thank you for your kindness. Bye, Henry."

Henry's face looked like he might cry. He just waved and shook his head. Over the months traveling on the wagon train, Elly had grown fond of Henry, and she could tell he felt the same way about her. She was going to miss working with him and their long discussions.

She watched them standing on the porch until the wagon went around the bend. Elly covered her face with her hands once Slim had driven onto the road.

"You gonna go in town and hire another woman to come take

SUNFLOWER BRIDE

care of Tate?" Henry asked, wiping his nose.

"Not for a while. I'm going to let the young fool realize how much Elly did for him. Maybe he'll learn a lesson."

"What kind of lesson?"

"He just might realize that he had a real jewel, but he didn't take good care of it." Major shook his head and walked toward the kitchen. "Come feed me. I'm starved."

Elly sobbed all the way back to town. Slim had never known a woman could shed so many tears. He tried to console her but he wasn't used to women. He never had a sister, only five brothers. His mama never cried when he was around. He couldn't wait to get this girl back to the rooming house.

He drove the wagon to the front gate of Mrs. Duffy's rooming house. Jumping off, he hurried around to Elly's side and helped her down. Although her eyes were puffy and red, he was going to miss seeing this beautiful lady every day.

"Thanks, Slim. Thanks for everything. You come and share our table when you're in town for supplies. Don't be a stranger, you hear?" Elly blew her nose, reached for her carpetbag and trudged into the house.

Two men stood in the parlor—one a fine dressed gentleman and the other a younger man. Once Elly's eyes adjusted to the dim light in the house, she screamed. "Timmy! My goodness, look at you."

Timmy stepped close to his sister, picked her up and swung her around and around. "I bet you're surprised to see me. Look, Preacher, she already has tears in her eyes she's so happy."

"Of course, I'm happy to see you. How long have you been here?"

"Only a little while. Reverend Cunningham and I came on the stage together from Brownsville, a town near the border."

"Is that where you've been since you got run . . . since you left Leesville months ago?"

"That's all right, sis. I told this preacher man my whole life story on the trip, ain't that right?" Timmy patted the preacher on the back.

"Well, almost. You failed to mention that you have a beautiful sister."

"Timmy," Elly began, but he stopped her. "I'm called Tim now, sis, not Timmy."

"Oh, of course you are, since you're a grown man. But listen to me. You don't address a minister by calling him preacher man. That is disrespectable."

"I understand and I won't do it again. Sorry, Padre. I will try to be more respectful in the future."

Elly sighed and shook her head. "Tim, where are you planning on staying, now that you're here in the big town of Sunflower?"

"Well, I was hoping to stay here, if Mrs. Duffy will let me. The padre here, I mean, Preacher Cunningham, is going to check out the church. He got a letter asking him to be the town's new preacher."

"Thank you, Tim, for explaining my future plans to your sister." He stepped around Tim and approached Elly. "You must excuse me for now, Miss Eddy, or is it Mrs.?

"Miss Eddy is correct . . . for now."

Well, that's nice." His sparkling eyes focused on Elly. "More than nice, I mean. I'd better get over to the church. I have a meeting with Mr. Johnson." He gave Elly a sweet smile. "I look forward to seeing you again." He placed his hat on his head and walked down the path to the boardwalk.

"Sis, are you engaged to someone?"

"No, why do you ask me that?"

"Well, you make it sound like you wouldn't be Miss Eddy for

long. I just thought you may have wedding plans in the future."

"No, no wedding plans, but Tim, that preacher friend of yours made me feel uncomfortable. He was looking at me like I was a juicy steak that he couldn't wait to eat."

"What? You're silly. Besides, how can you say that about a total stranger? He was just being nice to you. I never seen him looking at other girls before, and we traveled a long ways to get here."

"Elly, Elly, is that you? Oh my goodness. You're home and Timmy is here, too. What a surprise." Mrs. Duffy ran down the stairs, out of breath.

"Yes, I'm home. Safe and sound, and I found this young man in your parlor," she said, looping her arm in his. "He's looking for a place to live while in town."

Mrs. Duffy placed her arms around Elly's waist. "You and I must have a long talk, but of course, Timmy will stay here with us," she said, a warm smile on her lips.

"What do you mean you're home safe? Has something happened that I should know about?" Tim asked, his eyebrows forming a V.

"You just got here. I'll tell you all about my little adventure later, but for now let's get you settled first." Elly gave her little brother another hug.

"Now, Timmy, since you just arrived in town, I will allow you to stay two weeks free of charge." Mrs. Duffy, always the little businesswoman, informed Tim of the rules at her rooming house.

"Two weeks should give you time to find a job. I can't afford freeloaders, you understand. After that time, your room will be three dollars a month, two dollars for your laundry and two dollars for meals. Seven dollars total. Does that sound fair to you?"

"I guess," he mumbled. Elly noticed the change in his demeanor. He was still a freeloader, she surmised.

"We want you with us, but if you can find cheaper accommodations, I'll understand." Mrs. Duffy led Timmy to the bottom of the stairs. "Take the first room to the right at the top of the stairs. Open your window and allow a breeze to flow through. Your sister and I are going to have a long overdue talk while you get settled. Dinner is at six."

Chapter 26

Elly and Mrs. Duffy waited until Timmy had gone up the stairs to his room before they headed into the kitchen to sit at the table. "I'll make us a cup of tea while we chat, dearie," said Mrs. Duffy.

"Now, that I'm home I don't want you waiting on me. I should be caring for you." Elly sat down looking like she had the weight of the world on her shoulders.

"Mattie has gone to the store to get our groceries. Johnny is in school. He's such a little dear and so smart. You tell me all about Mr. Maynard's son. How is he doing?"

"He's in a bad way, again. He was almost healed until he fell off his horse," Tears spilled down her cheeks. "I nearly killed him."

"Stop right there and start from the beginning. Now I know about that old cowboy that shot Tate and kidnapped you. He's in jail waiting for the circuit judge to come. They will have his trial right here in town."

"Oh, no." Elly placed her hand over her heart. "That means I'll have to stand in front of the whole town and testify against him."

"Well, you'll probably be seated in a chair next to the judge's table, I believe."

"Mrs. Duffy," Elly leaped out of the chair. "You know what I mean. They'll ask me questions. They'll want to know what he did to me or didn't do, while alone with him in that line shack." Elly shook her head. "He didn't do anything bad to me. Just scared me mostly and tied me up."

"Child, you will be fine. You'll handle it just like you're handling all the talk about you and young Mr. Maynard."

"What do you mean?" Elly slipped back down in her chair. "What talk? Is someone talking about me caring for Tate? You were here when Major asked me to go to their ranch. We were never alone . . . together. I just don't understand people."

Mrs. Duffy sat drinking her tea and peered at Elly. "The men are talking about you and Tate being found together in the cave. You know, sleeping together. Last night, old Mr. Watts, a new boarder of ours, by the way. He's a nice man who likes to sit on the back porch and whittle wood. He made me a big wooden spoon and I love it—"

"Mrs. Duffy, please. Get back to what you were saying about the men discussing me and Tate."

"Sorry," she said. "Well, he told me that he overheard men planning a shivaree. A pretty wild one at that."

Elly jumped from her chair and strode to the back porch. She rubbed her backside and moaned. "What? I haven't heard anything about me and Tate. When did all this gossip start?"

"I was in the dry goods store when the posse came into town. Mr. Jackson was laughing with a couple of men and announced to his wife that you had been found. Of course, I was thrilled. Then he told his wife and me that we'd better get our best clothes ready because there was going to be a wedding soon. He said that you and Mr. Maynard would be getting hitched."

"Oh, my goodness," Elly said lowering herself into a kitchen chair. "I wonder if Tate has heard these rumors about us." Elly held her face in her hands. "Oh, Mrs. Duffy, Tate was nearly healed until I pulled him off his horse, and he broke open the stitches on his shoulder. When he fell, he was in so much pain he passed out. Nothing happened in that cave between us. I sat beside him most of the night. Almost most of the night. He woke up and he was cold. I built up the fire again, but he pulled me over into his arms because he was shivering. "Get me warm," he begged. "I was so tired from sitting beside him and cold too, so I fell asleep lying next to him. Later, the men came and took us to Tate's ranch."

"Why did you come back to town if Mr. Maynard still needs you to attend him?" Mrs. Duffy asked.

"We had a little disagreement. Sort of, anyway. No one would understand but me and him. I just felt that he would be better off without me. Everything I do is wrong." Both ladies didn't speak for a few minutes. "Major will find Tate another nurse."

"What are you going to do about those ugly rumors being spread about you two? Do you think you'll get married?"

"For now, nothing. We're innocent of any wrongdoing, and I will not be forced into a loveless marriage with anyone. I don't believe you could hold a gun on Tate and force him into doing anything he didn't want to do."

"I think I hear Mattie coming in the front gate. I'd better help her with the groceries," Mrs. Duffy said and pushed up from her seat.

"Please, Mrs. Duffy, I will help her. You just sit." Elly needed to keep busy and she was eager to see Mattie.

"Elly," Mattie screamed. "Oh, it so good to see you. When did you get here?" She carried a box of groceries into the kitchen.

"Do you have more that I can help you with?"

"Yes, but Joe is carrying the other box. He was right behind me. I must have closed the door in his face."

Joe appeared in the parlor and grinned at Elly. "Howdy, Miss," he said and jerked his old hat off his six-foot frame. He had a wide smile and a head of brown curls. He placed the box down on the dining room table, all the while gazing at Elly with puppy-dog eyes.

"Hello, yourself, young man. Thanks for helping Mattie with the supplies." She reached for her bag and pulled out a nickel. "Here you are," Elly said.

"Thanks. If I can do anything else for you, just ask. I'll be glad to help . . . you." He turned, nearly knocking a lantern off the hall table. He kept glancing back over his shoulder at Elly until he left the house.

"Mercy, he was shore moonstruck over you, Elly. He never acted like that around me."

"Goodness, he's just a kid. He's never seen me before, I guess."

"Oh, Elly, are you all right? Did that man hurt you before he got caught? I heard that Mr. Maynard got hurt again while out searching for you. Is he going to be all right?"

Elly didn't know which question to answer first.

"Listen to me. I am not giving you a minute to answer me. Come and let's put these supplies away and have a snack before I start lunch for heaven knows how many people we may have. Business is good, maybe too good." Mattie said with a giggle.

"Now that I'm back, I can help with the workload," Elly said.

"Won't you be leaving here soon . . . getting married and all?"

Elly peered at Mattie, then glanced at Mrs. Duffy. "No, I am not marrying anyone. Tate and I did nothing wrong, and the good people of Sunflower will have to find someone else to talk about."

"I didn't mean to upset you." Mattie looked worried. She probably heard the nasty rumors from the old biddies of the town.

"Listen, Mattie, while you were gone to the store, my brother arrived on the morning stage and he's upstairs in his room. He'll be staying with us for little while. His name is Tim, and he's twenty-one years old."

"That's great. I know you've been worried about him. I look forward to meeting him."

While Elly was preparing pies for the guests for lunch and dinner, Mattie was cutting dumplings to be dropped in the chicken broth that Mrs. Duffy had simmering on the stove. The chicken was cooked and cooling. Later Mattie would place the chicken back in the pot along with the dumplings to cook. A large pot of dried lima beans with slices of ham was simmering while pans of cornbread baked in the oven. Lunch was a simple fare, but dinner offered many dishes to choose from each day.

Elly opened the back door to allow a cool breeze into the kitchen when she saw Major and Tate parked behind the house. She stepped out on the porch and watched Major help Tate down from the wagon. Tate's complexion was as white as a dove on a snowy roof, and he looked like he was ready to kill someone.

"What in hades are you doing here, and why aren't you home in bed? Are you trying to kill yourself?" Elly stood with her hands on her hips, waiting for the men to come inside.

"No, I have you to do that for me. Get out of my way so I can go to my old bed and lie down. If my nurse won't stay with me at the ranch, I have to come to her." He growled and marched past her straight to her room.

"Major, how could you allow him to ride here in that wagon? Have you hired him another nurse?"

"He wouldn't let me ask another lady to help. He said you did this to him, so you can take care of him, even if he had to come to you."

"Lord, help me," Elly mumbled. "There will be plenty of talk now."

"Yep, I told him so, but he said he didn't care. Please take good care of him. At least, old Doc Weaver is close at hand."

"Elly," Tate yelled.

"He's been a bear since you left. I think he misses you, even if he never admits it."

Elly glanced at Major and said, "Just like old times." She smiled at him and walked down the hall to help Tate get settled in bed.

"Yes, Lord and Master. How may I help you?" She leaned against the door. He wiggled his finger at her and pointed to the side of the bed. "Don't be smug."

She took a noticeable breath and slowly eased over to him.

"Why in the hell did you leave the ranch when you knew I needed you?" he growled. "I know you didn't mean to make me fall off my horse, but I did, and I was sure I was dying."

"I know. You said that I almost managed to kill you." She sucked in her breath and held back a nasty comment. "How do you think that made me feel?" Tears clouded her eyes, but she bit down on her bottom lip. This fool had made her cry for the last time.

"Elly," he called her name so softly that a shiver traveled down her spine. "I don't blame you, really, but I need your help. Please, help me . . . by removing my boots."

"Oh, you," Elly laughed and went to the foot of the bed. She pulled off his boots and socks, then gently rubbed each ankle.

"Oh, that feels so good. No other woman would do that for me," he said, closing his eyes.

Elly picked up a roll of gauze and lifted his shirt front. "I'd better check your shoulder wound before you go to sleep. Are you hungry?"

"Am I alive?" he said, making her laugh again.

"I never knew a man could eat as much as you do and not get fat. Let me check you over, then I'll bring you a bowl of chicken and dumplings. You need to rest after riding in that wagon."

Elly left Tate resting on her bed and strolled back into the kitchen. Major was still sitting at the table. "Did you remember to bring Tate's medicine with you?"

"Yes, but he didn't take any this morning. That young fool is hurting but he'll never tell you." New lines had formed on Major's forehead and around his mouth.

"Would you like to lie down in one of our empty rooms upstairs before lunch? You look exhausted."

"No, I have a list of supplies to pick up for Henry. I'll go and take care of that, and after lunch I'd better get back to the ranch. So, Miss Elly, will you care for Tate?"

Elly smiled at the wonderful man who had been so good to her from the night she lost everything in the Leesville's fire. "How can I refuse you?" She walked him to the front door.

"Major, you probably heard the ugly talk about Tate and me. We did nothing wrong. Tate and I haven't discussed it, but we will. I will not be forced into a marriage, and I know Tate won't either. I just hope that those people will find something else to talk about soon."

"Please don't fret over the gossip. The big trial will be coming up soon, and that will take their minds off you two. I'll be back in about a half an hour."

Elly knew that Tate needed some medicine to help relieve his pain, but he also needed good nourishment to help heal. Besides, he was as hungry as a bear on a diet. Once he had some food, she would force the medicine down him if she had to.

After an early lunch of chicken and dumplings and cornbread, he took the foul-tasting medicine and went to sleep. He must have been in pain because he didn't put up an argument.

Chapter 27

Later that evening, Tim came into the kitchen. "Hi, sis, look who I brought to dinner tonight." Tim stepped aside to let the preacher into the kitchen.

Good evening, Miss Eddy. I hope you don't mind me coming without an invitation?" he said, giving Elly a sly smile.

"Please tell me your name again, Preacher?" Elly was ill at ease around this man for some unknown reason, and she didn't want him to think she remembered him from this morning.

"Scott Cunningham, Madam, or Preacher Cunningham. Whatever you wish to call me."

Oh, yes. Preacher Cunningham, this is Mrs. Duffy's Rooming House and we serve three meals a day to our boarders and other people of the town. You don't have to have an invitation. Our meals are fifty cents, but tonight you are our guest."

"Thank you. I appreciate your hospitality, and it is nice to know that a young single man like myself will have a place to enjoy a home-cooked meal."

"Tim, take the preacher into the dining room and find seats at the table. We will serve dinner in just a few minutes."

The preacher left, but Tim stayed behind. "Sis, Preacher Scott needs a nice place to stay. Can he let a room here until the townspeople fix up his little house?"

"No, I'm sorry, Tim. We have a full house." Elly hated to tell a little white lie to her brother, but the thought of that young preacher in the same house would ruin her nerves.

"But, Sis, there's two empty rooms upstairs."

"No. Those rooms are reserved for guests who will be here tomorrow. Sorry. I am sure the townspeople will find him a suitable place to stay. Besides, Tim, you aren't his caretaker."

"Elly," Tate called from the doorway of her bedroom.

"Who's that?" Tim pointed at Tate, who stood barefooted with his shirt open, in dire need of a shave.

"That's my patient. I'm his nurse. Now you, young man, please go and take a seat at the table, and I'll introduce you to Tate in a little while."

Tate plodded into the kitchen and watched as the young man left. "That young fellow thinks I'm your lover."

"What? Of course, he doesn't, "Elly said laughing. "That handsome young man is my brother, Timmy. He just arrived this morning on the stage."

"The same young man who stole all your money?"

"Well, he did do that. I'm surprised you remembered," she said stirring a big bowl of peas. "I'm praying that he's changed. He likes to gamble, just like my pa always did, but I hope he learned his lesson in Leesville. He'll be looking for a job tomorrow."

"If I put on my boots, may I eat at the table?"

Elly examined him from his head to his toes. "If you button up your shirt and let me comb your hair. You could use a shave, but we'll let that slide for now. Dinner is about ready to be served."

"Oh, how stupid of me to think that I could be comfortable in the presence of your customers," Tate said without a smile.

Mattie placed a tray of meatloaf, a big bowl of chicken and dumplings, a large platter of baked pork chops along with mashed potatoes, turnip greens, field peas and cornbread on the table while Mrs. Duffy served coffee, tea or milk to each guests.

Elly tapped on her glass and got everyone's attention. "I would like to introduce my brother, Tim. Also, our town is pleased to have a new preacher, Scott Cunningham, joining us tonight and many of you already know Tate Maynard. Mr. Maynard will be staying with us until he is healed."

Tim requested that the new preacher ask the blessing. With dramatic flair, he thanked God for bringing him to this wonderful town where he might find a life partner. Everyone sat still as the night, and then several of the men laughed and the ladies giggled. "Let's hope you will find happiness here, dear boy," Mrs. Duffy commented.

Everyone began passing the food around the table. Tate opened his eyes during the last part of the blessing, and he noticed the preacher was staring at Elly when he spoke about marriage.

"Mr. Maynard," Mrs. Langley said, "are you the young man who got shot by that man who's in our jail?"

"I'm sorry, madam. Have we met before?" Tate asked, irritated by the woman's interest.

"Oh, I don't think so." She giggled a little behind her napkin. "I came to help Mrs. Duffy when Elly had to leave for a while. Now that she's back, I'm hoping that I'll be able to stay on here every day." The girl glanced at Mrs. Duffy.

"Of course, we need you to work for us. With as many customers and boarders as we have now, we need all the help I can afford to hire."

"I understand from Mr. Johnson that there is a man in jail that may hang for attempted murder. Who did he try to kill?" Preacher Cunningham asked, scanning each face around the table.

"Preacher Cunningham, please. Let's talk about something more pleasant at the table. Why don't you tell us where you came from and how you became a man of God?"

"I'm from Brownsville. I had a small church, but it burned to the ground. My pa was a preacher and I was raised as a preacher's kid. It was natural I'd become a man of God, too." He flashed a smile at everyone sitting around the table and, but his eyes lingered on Elly who was busy cutting the bread.

Tate raised his eyebrows at the preacher's comments. He could tell that the man didn't like him for some reason. "Tim," Tate said, "Your sister says that you will be looking for a job tomorrow. Have you worked on a ranch before?"

"No, sir," he said, "I helped on a cattle drive after I left Leesville. We drove a big herd to Mexico. Does that count?"

"It would depend on what you did on the drive. But driving cattle on the range is long, hard work," Tate said.

"It was boring. Hot during the day, cold at night, and the ground was hard. I did have a nice ramrod boss and the other men were decent. The pay wasn't bad." He scratched his neck. "I'd like something a little more settled."

"If you can't find something here in town, I am sure my pa would hire you to work on our big spread. We have retired here in Sunflower and have a ranch about seven miles south of here. We're planting our fields and branding over two-hundred head of cattle. Good help is always needed." Tate glanced at Elly who was busy replacing bowls of food on the table.

"Thank you, sir. I will remember your offer." Tim smiled at the preacher.

Later that evening, as Elly carried in the laundry from the clothesline, Tate was sitting in the swing on the back porch.

"You should be resting. You are too weak to be sitting up for so long, especially out here in the damp air." Elly placed her basket down on the porch and positioned herself beside him.

"I wanted a breath of fresh air." Tate gave the swing a little push with his toe. Elly relaxed while listening to the chirping of the birds and the sounds of crickets settling in for the night.

"You know, in all the time I've known you, I've never heard you speak about your pa before. I heard you say that you had taken over your mom's laundry business, but that's all. Why don't you tell me about your childhood while your parents were alive?"

"My life wasn't as nice as yours, I'm sure about that. Your pa is good to you, even now that you're grown."

"Yes, and I had a wonderful mama. She died way too young."

"My mama was a good woman, too, and she loved Timmy and me. She worked herself to death trying to care for us. My pa is still alive, somewhere. He walked away from our rented house and never returned." She said softly. "Timmy and I were thrilled when he left because when he came home drunk, he beat our mother. When Mama heard him coming home, she hurried us outside or told me to lock our bedroom door. She protected us from his drunken rages. I never understood why he wanted to hurt the woman he swore to love and the mother of his children. She was a good woman who cooked, slaved over hot wash water and steaming irons to help with the bills."

"What kind of job did your pa have?" Tate's brow furrowed.

"He was a bartender at Wild Bill's Saloon for years. I was told he started drinking and flirting with the ladies who worked there. When they refused him, he took his anger out on Mama. I didn't know this until after she died." Elly sighed and leaned back on the swing.

"I'm sorry you and Tim had a rough time as children."

"When mama was alive, she insisted I go to school and learn to read and write. She was so proud of me. When I came home, I helped with her business by delivering the laundry and cooking pies. She was the best pie maker in town and she taught me. We made pies for the bakery and the boardinghouse in town. On weekends, I tutored a few younger students with their ciphering and reading. Tutoring didn't pay much, but I was able to give mama some extra money."

"How old were you when your mama passed?" he asked.

"Seventeen. I continued with her business for nearly three years. Once Timmy refused to help me with the deliveries, I made him move out of our house. Later, the school board needed someone to fill in as a schoolteacher because they couldn't get an answer to their ads requesting one. Soon after I took the job, my little house was placed up for sale, so I moved in with Mrs. Duffy. She let me continue to make pies, but I had to give up my laundry business."

"So you've lived with Mrs. Duffy for several years, is that right? After the fire, you said you would work for us if Mrs. Duffy was allowed to travel with us. You two are close."

"Yes, she was good to me, and she tolerated Tim. She wouldn't allow him to live at the boardinghouse because he couldn't pay the rent. He went to work over at Wild Bill's where he rented a room over the saloon." Elly remembered the night of the fire when Timmy was driven out of town on a rail for cheating at cards.

"Mrs. Duffy is a businesswoman, so although we were close, she didn't get involved in my personal life. She and I have gotten closer on the trip here, and I've learned to care about her like the grandmother I never had."

Tate leaned forward. "I feel like I know you a little better now. You're an independent woman who learned early to stand on her own, even though you're a city girl."

Noticing that Tate was frowning each time he moved his shoulder, she stood. "All right, mister. You've had enough fresh air. Time we get ready for bed."

"Sounds like a good idea to me. Do you sleep on the right or left side?" He asked, a teasing grin on his face.

"What? Oh, you. You'd better not let anyone hear you talking to me like that. We'll be standing in front of the new preacher whether we want to are not."

"Speaking about being forced into marriage, I know you've heard the gossip about us. I heard it too. Listen, I have strong feelings for you," he said, gripping her hand in his. "But I don't want to start off my life with a woman who was forced into marrying me. Do you understand?"

Elly shook loose of his hold on her hand. "That's the same way I feel. We didn't do anything wrong, and I am not going into a loveless marriage with anyone."

Tate stood, giving her a wide berth, he opened the back screen door for her. "Good, we both feel the same way."

Elly entered the kitchen, then spun around, nearly hitting Tate in the chest before she caught herself. "I forgot the wash on the porch. Excuse me." Tate stepped out of her way, then disappeared down the hall.

She gathered her emotions and pasted a sweet smile on her face as she entered Tate's room. "Here, lift your foot while I take off your boot." She removed the triangle cloth and unbuttoned his shirt. Placing it on the back of a chair, she averted her eyes as he shuffled out of his jeans. He sat down on the bed while she adjusted the sheet and quilt over the lower part of his tall frame. They did this all without saying a word, though the air was filled with tension.

"Let me check your bandage," she finally said. "I don't see any blood on the outside, but I need to make sure the stitches are holding and there's no sign of infection." After removing the bandages and replacing fresh gauze, the two wounds looked like they were healing well. "Do you need any pain medicine? The doc said only take it if you feel like you need it." Elly closed the window. The fall air was a lot colder now, and she didn't want Tate to get chilled during the night.

"I'll try to sleep without it tonight. I hate the way it makes me feel when I wake up." As Elly moved to leave his room, he said, "I guess you know you have a new admirer. That new preacher kid is sniffing after you already."

"Tate, you say the most awful things. No one is *sniffing* after me, as you put it."

"Well, you'd better be careful around that wet-nosed preacher."

Elly sighed and made no comment. She turned off his lantern and patted his quilt one more time. "Good night. The lantern on the stove will give you light if you need to go to the water closet during the night."

She hummed on her way to her room. "Mr. Tate is a little jealous, just maybe."

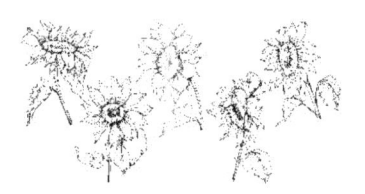

Chapter 28

During the night, Elly heard a clash. It sounded like a chair had slammed to the floor or someone was stumbling around in the house. She jumped up and grabbed her umbrella. Easing her door open, she listened.

"Damnit," she heard a familiar voice say.

"Tate?" she whispered, "Is that you?"

"Yes, who else would be up this time of the night? I need pain medicine. Where have you put it?" he growled.

"Oh, mercy. Let me help you back to bed." He was walking around the kitchen in his long johns, barefooted. He had lowered the top part of his long johns below his waist. Dark hair showed from below his navel. Heavens, he was a sight.

Elly covered him up and told him she would be right back. "I'm hungry, too. Get me a piece of pie and some milk, please." Even with his growl, he sounded so pitiful that she did as he asked. After he had eaten his treat, she gave him a big dose of medicine.

"Now you should be able to relax and rest. Do you need anything else before I go back to my room?"

Giving Elly his plate, he cast her a cocky grin. He was so darn charming. If he knew that she would love to slide in the bed and sleep up against his hard, warm body, they'd both be in trouble. She remembered the night in the cave and she wanted more, but that was not to be.

Two days later, Tim slinked into the back door of the rooming house where Tate and Elly sat at the kitchen table. She was peeling apples while he nibbled on pieces and drank a cup of coffee.

"Howdy, sis, Mr. Maynard," Tim said and lowered himself into a chair at the table. "Mr. Maynard, I was wondering if that job offer you talked about on your ranch is still open. I can't find any work in town and I shore need work," Tim said, looking forlorn and weary.

Tate glanced at Elly, and she nodded. "Timmy, Tim, I mean. You know ranching is hard work. Those men work from sunup to sundown, and they don't ride into town but once a week," Elly said.

"Elly," Tate reached for her hand and gave it a tight squeeze. "I believe your brother was speaking to me about a job."

"Of course, he was but I just wanted him to know . . . Oh, all right. I'll go and check the wash outside while you men talk." She stood and disappeared out the door.

"Since you have worked on a cattle drive, you know that working with cattle is hard work. We have other things on my ranch that need attending to besides just branding and carrying feed out to the herd. We have fields that need plowing and planting, hogs to slop and keep clean as possible, goats that need milking because we sell the milk to several farmers who make cheese. There are many small jobs on the ranch that need someone's attention daily. You won't get bored if you like to be outside. I have a good cook who prepares three square meals a day and a comfortable bunkhouse for my men. I pay forty dollars a month and later, if a man proves to be a good worker, I pay more." Tate watched Tim's reaction. "Is this something you would like to try?"

"Sounds great to me, but there is one thing. I don't own a horse or any gear."

"That won't be a problem. Slim, my foreman, will help you choose a horse. There's one thing more. I ask that you work for me for thirty days. If you can't carry your load or if you just don't like working on the ranch, you walk away, and there will be no hard feelings. How does that sound to you?"

Elly came back inside and washed her hands. "Sorry, men, but I must finish my apples and get my pies in the oven."

"Sis, you are now looking at a new cowboy on the Maynard Ranch," he said proudly. "When do you want me to start?"

"How about today?" Tate said. "I'm afraid you're going to have to purchase some new clothes to work in. Your sister practically wore your other clothes out on the trip here from Leesville."

Tim's eyes grew big and he glanced at Elly, whose face was on fire. "Oh, you," she shook her head at Tate. "You know I had nothing else to wear." Both of them laughed, but her brother just looked on, not understanding what was funny.

"I tell you what, Tim. You go over to the dry goods store and pick up several pairs of jeans, a new belt, sturdy boots, and several shirts. Tell Mr. Wilson to put them on my tab. A cowboy can't work in your fancy duds, now can he?"

After Tim left for the store, Elly sat and chopped more apples. "Thank you. I hope he won't be a disappointment. I think working out of town will be good for him."

"Between my pa and Slim, he won't have time to think about playing cards. My men play some but only bet matchsticks."

"That will certainly be a change for him," Elly laughed.

"You know you need to do that more," Tate commented.

"Do what . . . more?" Elly smoothed back her hair.

"Laugh. You're a beautiful woman." He stood. "I'm going to lie back down. Do you want to tuck me in?" His eyebrows bobbed up and down.

"No, Mr. Maynard. You're a big boy now and you'll manage

just fine, but take it easy."

The young preacher was making his rounds in the town. He chatted with all the business owners and invited everyone to attend his first church service. Preacher Scott was making a lasting impression on the ladies.

Since the last minister left, the little house next to the church had needed repair, and the ladies of Sunflower had taken it upon themselves to fix it up. They encouraged their husbands and store owners to donate their time and money to make the parsonage look like an inviting place to live. They built a new porch with a swing and put on a new roof. Inside, they installed a new stove, brought in a bed and mattress, a rocker and a kitchen table. The small fireplace and chimney were as good as new.

Several of the ladies made curtains and donated quilts and pillows to cover the new bed. A new lantern sat in the middle of the table and cooking supplies and canned goods lined the new cabinets. The young preacher wouldn't need for anything as long as he flashed his handsome smile on the ladies.

Saturday evening before his first church service, the preacher came to dinner at Mrs. Duffy's Rooming House. "Hello, Miss Eddy. I hope you don't mind me joining you for supper tonight?" he asked, giving her his most winsome smile.

"You won't be just joining me, sir, but of course, we are happy to have you anytime. Please go in the parlor and take a seat. Mattie is placing the food on the table now."

"May I help you in the kitchen with anything?" He blocked her exit from the doorway.

"Please, Preacher. Just place your hat on the rack and take a seat. I have everything under control." She flashed him a smile in return, but hers didn't reach her eyes. She darted past him into the kitchen.

As the young preacher sat down next to Mrs. Wilson, the store owner's wife, he gave her a sweet smile.

"Oh, Preacher Cunningham, I cannot wait to hear your first sermon. What will your topic be for our congregation?"

"Matrimony, the sacrament of marriage." He said loud enough for everyone at the table to hear.

"Why have you chosen to speak about marriage?" she asked.

"I understand that many of the couples in town and surrounding areas have been married only a few weeks, and most of the ladies were mail-order brides. This will be a good time to let the newlyweds know the importance of marriage."

The room became silent, and someone asked if he would say grace. All heads bowed and he offered the blessing with flourish.

As soon as he finished, he looked into Elly's eyes. She could tell he was smitten, but he still made her uneasy. She had no feelings for this handsome young man, and she hoped that another girl would soon gain his attention.

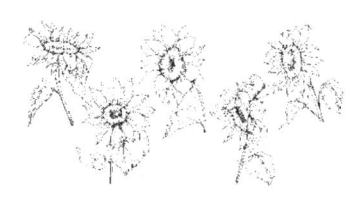

Chapter 29

Early the next morning, Elly, Mrs. Duffy, Mattie and Johnny all dressed in their Sunday best, were preparing to leave for church when Tate called Elly's name.

"All of you go ahead and save me a seat. The church will have a packed house today, but I need to see what Tate wants." She watched the trio walk out of the house, then hurried into Tate's bedroom. "What can I do for you? I'm heading out to church this morning."

"I know. I think I can go home today. My wounds are closed up good and I can use my right arm now. Pa will be at church this morning. Tell him to come and get me."

"Maybe, but I should have the doctor come and look at you one more time. I'm not sure you're ready to care for yourself." She bit down on her bottom lip.

"You know," he said, "I was thinking about going to church with you. I can walk over there, and if I get tired, I'll come back here. I can sit in the back with some of the other fellows. I'd kinda like to hear that young man."

"Of course, I'm not your jailer, as you have called me. If you want to go, let me get you some clothes and help you dress . . . for the last time." She mumbled.

While Elly hurried down the aisle to sit with Mrs. Duffy and Mattie, Tate sat on the back pew, breathing hard. The walk was almost too much for him, but he'd never admit it. His pa raised his eyebrows when their eyes met but remained seated. Slim gave Tate a nod to let him know that he had seen him, too.

After the opening hymns, everyone eased back into their pews and waited for the mayor to come to the lectern.

"It gives me great pleasure to introduce our new parson to our fine community. He told me all of you have already made him feel right at home. And I thank you for doing that. Now, I know you didn't come to listen to me prattle on and on, so without any further words, I give you Preacher Scott Cunningham." Everyone clapped and cheered as the mayor took his seat.

The new preacher walked to the front of the church dressed in a black robe. A small white collar peeked from under the robe, and a gold cross hung from his neck. He cut a handsome figure with his blond hair slicked back. He stood tall and scanned his new congregation until he saw Elly. His eyes lingered on her until people craned their necks to see who he zeroed in on.

Elly felt her face blush a fiery red. The nerve of the man, thought Elly. She wanted to bolt out of the pew and leave, but that would only draw more attention to herself. She hoped Tate had not witnessed the man looking at her like she was part of his sermon.

Her wish didn't come true. Tate and the whole congregation witnessed the new preacher staring at Elly and smiling at her as if they were the only people in the church. She cast a backwards glance at Tate. His eyes were so narrowed she could tell he was having a hard time holding his anger in check.

The young preacher's voice boomed over his new

congregation. "Today, I have chosen to talk to you about matrimony—the union between a man and a woman. Since I arrived in Sunflower, I have learned that so many of you have just said your vows, and to strangers at that. I feel that since many of you are newlyweds, you should understand the importance of what you have done. Marriage is not something you take lightly."

"You're a little late for this sermon, Preacher. The deed is done." One of the old men called out, and all the men in the congregation laughed.

"I know you're right, sir, but it doesn't hurt to tell these couples or anyone else who may be thinking about marriage a few things God said about this union." Everyone quieted down, and the old fellow took his seat, grinning.

The young preacher spoke on the importance of knowing one's mate's likes and dislikes before agreeing to marry. "It is good to want the same things out of life and have a strong commitment to that person." As he talked, he quoted a scripture from Matthew 19:5, 6: "—for this cause shall a man leave father and mother, and shall cleave to his wife: and they twain shall be one flesh, wherefore they are no more twain, but one flesh. What therefore God hath joined together, let not man put asunder."

He continued, "As we depart this morning I want to send you away with a couple phrases God said about love. He said in Ephesians 4:2-3, 'Be completely humble and gentle; be patient, bearing with one another in love. Make every effort to keep the unity of the Spirit through the bond of peace.' And last he said in John 15:12, 'This is my commandment, that you love one another as I have loved you.' I pray that I will see you next Sunday if not before. Amen."

The preacher stepped down from the pulpit and headed as fast and hurried to the front doors of the church, wanting to speak with each person and shake the men's hands. He hoped to hear praises about his sermon, and he wasn't disappointed from the ladies.

Elly stood on her tiptoes trying to see if Tate had made it out of the church before the crowd gathered around him. She didn't want anyone to bump into him and cause pain to his sore body.

Major took her arm and stepped into the aisle. "I'm coming to the rooming house for lunch. I can't believe I saw Tate in the back pew."

"I know, but he wanted to come. He says that he's going home with you today. He'll be fine at home with you and Henry helping out when needed."

"Come on, I will walk you back to the rooming house." Tate was waiting for them toward the back. "Oh, there you are, son."

As they made their way to the door of the church, the preacher grabbed Elly's hand before she could step out of his reach.

"I was so pleased to see you in the congregation this morning, Miss Elly. Did you enjoy my sermon? I was hoping you would get the message about love," he whispered so close to her ear, it tickled, but not in a nice way.

"We all got the message loud and clear, preacher boy. I want you to leave this little filly alone. Got it? She's already spoken for." Tate shouted loud enough for the bystanders to overhear him.

Elly sucked in her breath and jumped off the front porch of the church, practically running across the street and down the boardwalk to the rooming house. She raced into her room and slammed the door, nearly rattling all the windowpanes.

In a few minutes, Tate pushed her door open. "All right, Miss High and Mighty. Get your fanny out here now so we can have a discussion."

She whirled around. "Fanny? Discussion?"

"Elly, Tate, please," said Mrs. Duffy. "We have a roomful of guests for Sunday dinner. Please keep it down."

Elly glared at Tate and motioned for him to come into her room. "How dare you call me a 'filly' and say that I have been spoken for." Before he could answer, she demanded, "Just who do I belong to, Mister?"

Tate reached out with his good arm and jerked her toward his chest. "Oh, that hurt," he cringed.

"Good, I hope it hurts like Hades," yet a smile crept across her face.

He pulled her closer and pressed her lips against his. Her arms came up around his neck, and he lifted her off the floor. Her breasts lay flat on his chest. Once he had her quiet, he forgot about all the pain she was causing him. Their kisses deepened, and they became lost in their own world. She whispered his name and tucked her head under his chin.

The pain was becoming too much for him so he let her slide to the floor. He leaned over and stared at her haunted eyes. "I'm sorry. The pain."

"Tate," Elly whispered, "Please just go home with your pa. I can't seem to resist you, and I can't do this anymore." Elly got to her feet, whirled around and left the room. She entered the water closet and locked the door.

Walking slowly back to his room, Major was sitting on his bed. "I packed your personal belongings. You ready to go?"

"Yes, it's for the best, for now."

"Mattie wrapped us up a couple of sandwiches to eat on the way home. Let's go." Major took his carpetbag and opened the back door. They headed to the livery and got their wagon.

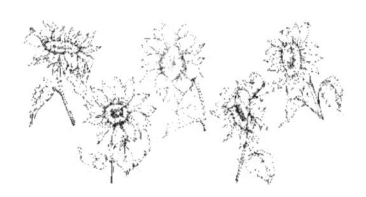

Chapter 30

Henry worked as fast as he could preparing breakfast for all the men. He really missed Elly's help and Miguel had not come back with his daughter. Major assigned the newest hand to help him out. The youngster wasn't happy having to work in the kitchen.

"I need those potatoes peeled, sonny. I have about twenty minutes before those hungry men come storming in here ready to eat."

"Hey, old man, I ain't no old woman who knows how to peel potatoes or wash dishes. I came out here to work on the ranch, not be kitchen help."

Tate stood at the kitchen door and listened to the spoiled brother of Elly's. "Tim, if you aren't happy here, you can go on back to town. The road is right out there."

"I like it here, really I do, but I ain't never had to do this kind of work. It's woman's work."

"Look at Henry. Is he a woman? No, he's not, but you haven't turned away any of the food he's prepared for us to eat. For now, Henry needs help and you are the last man hired, so you're elected." Tate stood and watched Tim decide what he wanted to do.

"All right, I understand. I'll do my best, but I won't have to do

SUNFLOWER BRIDE

this the whole time I am working here, will I?"

"No, son, you won't. Major is trying to hire a woman to work for us. Maybe he'll have someone in a day or two. Henry," Tate said, "give me a pan of those potatoes so I can help." Henry and Tim glanced at him, and both men grinned. "Sure, boss."

After breakfast, Tate helped Henry wash the dishes, then he sent Tim out to gather and wash the eggs. "Henry, I'm going to my office to check up on my paperwork. I'll come in and help you with lunch. I really don't want Tim to quit this job. He needs it, and Elly will be upset with him, and I don't want that."

Slim came into the office carrying a paper. "Hey, boss, a young messenger rode out here with this note. He says it's from the sheriff. The boy said that the circuit judge will be arriving tomorrow."

"Tomorrow? That's a lot sooner than I thought." Tate said.

"Yep, this is going to upset Elly something awful," Slim said.

"What do you mean? Why will she be upset?" Tate shifted papers to a different pile on his desk.

Slim sat in one of the soft chairs and got comfortable. "She told me one evening she was terrified about having to testify against that Bill Sawyer. Elly said the judge would ask her what he did while he held her kidnapped. She told me he didn't hurt her in any way, but she's still scared to have to be put on the witness stand. She doesn't want to be part of the cause of his death."

"I don't think the judge will order him to be hanged. He didn't kill me."

"I'm just telling you how Elly feels." Slim got up and walked to the office door. "Let me know if you want me to drive you into town."

Tate unfolded the note from the sheriff. *Come to my office as soon as possible. Bill Sawyer wants to talk to you before the judge gets here. Maybe he will plead guilty and there won't be a trial.*

Sheriff Murray.

Tate walked into the kitchen and asked Henry if he would round up Slim for him. "Tell him I'm ready to go into town. If you have a list of supplies you need, give it to him while I change clothes."

A few hours later, Tate walked into Sheriff Murray's office.

Slim drove the horse and wagon down to the livery and jumped off. "Goodness, Miss Mattie, I nearly leaped right on top of you."

"Oh hello, Slim. How are you doing?" She looked around him. "Did you come to town alone?"

"No, I brought Tate into town to see the sheriff. It seems Bill Sawyer wants to talk with him. There I go, running off at the mouth. Please don't say anything about this. Tate is going to fire me one day for telling his business."

"Don't fret. I'll keep this to myself. I do hope something good will come out of this visit. Elly is so worried about the trial."

"I know. She told me, and this morning I told Tate that Elly was scared of having to testify."

"How is Tim doing? Is he happy working on the ranch?"

"Not sure if he's happy, but he's a good worker. For a while he's helping Henry, the chuck wagon cook, who works for Tate in the kitchen. Not many men like that job, but Major is trying to hire a lady to come out to the ranch and work. There's a shortage of women in Sunflower."

"Really? I wonder if the pay is good. I sure could use a better paying job, but the school is so close and Johnny is happy."

"You could speak with Major about the job. There was one family who lived on the place and their sons rode into town to attend school. That was before Tate and his pa finally took over their ranch."

"Thanks, Slim. I'll speak with Major, but please keep quiet about this. I haven't told Mrs. Duffy that I am looking for a better paying job. She has been so good to me, but I work from morning to night for room and board with little pay."

"My lips are sealed," said Slim and led the horse into the barn.

"Good afternoon, Sheriff," Tate said.

"Howdy, young man. Glad you could come so quickly. My prisoner has about walked a hole in my cell floor waiting for you to arrive. Come on back. I'll have to lock you in the cell with him, is that all right?"

"Sure, I'm not afraid of him." He followed the sheriff behind the office toward two cells, one empty and one occupied.

"Sawyer, here's the guest you requested. Be on your best behavior, you hear?"

Tate entered the cell and ambled to the small window where prisoners could view the main street. "Not much to see out this window," Tate said to break the tension between him and Sawyer.

"You want to sit, Mr. Maynard?" Sawyer gestured with his head.

"I'll stand. Let's get on with this visit, so tell me what you want to talk about."

"It's like this, Maynard. I've been thinking. Your woman, that Miss Eddy, is the real reason I got so upset the night you and I had our tussle. She had refused to let me marry Mattie. I know I was drinking. She got me riled, and I said I'd just take her as my bride. Well, you showed up and hit me. You know the rest."

"You said you'd been thinking about this. What are your thoughts about the argument between you and Miss Eddy?"

"If I'm going to hang, I can make her very sorry for what she did to me. We were together overnight in the line shack, and I can destroy her reputation so bad that no man would every want to marry the little slut."

Tate's fists were clenched so tight his nails were digging into his hands. What he wouldn't do to put his fist through Sawyer's smirking face. Instead he said, "I don't believe the circuit judge will sentence you to hang. You might get a long prison sentence, but—"

Before he finished his sentence, Bill Sawyer came nose to nose with him and yelled, "I don't want to go to prison, man. You don't understand what I want."

"Tell . . . me. Spit is out now, before I lose my patience," Tate demanded.

"Drop the attempted murder charge against me. I was drunk and wanted to hurt somebody, and you just happened to be in my way. That Eddy woman is who I should have shot. She's the cause of my trouble. Just let me out of this jail and I'll get a fresh start somewhere else."

"What about your farm? I remember you said it was yours free and clear."

"I want you to buy it. Give me five hundred dollars, and everything that is out there will be yours, lot, stock and barrel."

"Five hundred dollars is a lot of money. You don't have more than fifty head of cattle and the house needs repair. I won't give you five hundred dollars, but I will offer you two hundred and fifty. I'm not sure it would be wise of me to drop the charges against you. You might try to hurt Miss Eddy," Tate said through narrowed eyes.

"No, I wouldn't do that. I give you my word," Sawyer said. "I'll take your offer, but you have to drop all the charges, and I can ride out of Sunflower a free man."

"Sheriff Murray," Tate called, "Please come in here."

The sheriff unlocked the door and stepped into the cell. "What's going on?" he asked.

"Draw up the papers to release this prisoner. I'm going to drop the charges against him, with his word that he will leave this territory. While you are drawing up your papers, I'll go across the street and bring the banker over here. Mr. Sawyer is selling me his farm, lot, stock and barrel today."

"Sit on your cot, Mr. Sawyer. This will take more than a few minutes." The sheriff and Tate walked back into his office.

"Are your sure this is what you want to do?"

"Yes. Miss Eddy's reputation is on the line. That fool's threatening to ruin her good name if he's placed on trial. He wasn't going to plead guilty so he could spread lies about her. She was scared to death to have to testify against him. It's for the best to let him go free. He isn't a bad man when he's sober. Besides, he's going to leave the area."

Sheriff Murray reached for a paper on his desk and glanced up at Tate. "I have just one more thing to ask you, son. When are you going to marry that gal?'

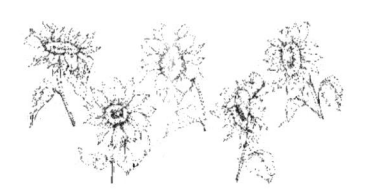

Chapter 31

Tate walked out of the sheriff's office with Bill Sawyer after signing the papers for the sale of his farm. Sawyer tucked the money into his pocket, then the sheriff escorted him to the livery. After Sawyer saddled his horse and rode out of town—forever, Tate hoped—he headed to Mrs. Duffy's Rooming House. Elly would be there, most likely baking pies.

"Howdy, Mr. Tate," said Johnny. "You know, we're gonna be moving to your ranch. I can hardly wait. Can I have my own horse?"

"Johnny," Mattie covered his little mouth. "Where did you hear that?"

"I heard you and Mr. Slim talking this morning. Ain't it true? Ain't you going to work for Major?" His innocent eyes held a hopeful glint.

"You run outside and play while I talk with Mr. Maynard."

"But mama, you can call him Mr. Tate like I do, can't she, Mr. Tate?" Johnny spouted as he walked backward out the front door.

Mattie hung her head. "I'm so embarrassed. I had no idea he was listening to my conversation with Slim."

"Is Elly in the kitchen," Tate smiled at her scarlet-red face.

"I think so. I was upstairs making up beds, but come on in."

"Let me talk with Elly, and then you and I can have a nice chat about the conversation Johnny overheard", Tate said.

Mattie nodded and rolled her eyes. "That child." She headed to the kitchen with Tate trailing behind her. "Elly, Tate is here and he wants to talk with you."

"Hello. Can you stop what you're doing and have a talk with me? I have some good news that I know you'll want to hear."

Elly wiped her hands on her apron, patted her hair and opened the back door. "Let's talk on the back porch. It's cooler out there."

"I know you've heard that the circuit judge will be in town tomorrow." He watched her reaction to his comment.

Elly shook her head and held her hands together in a tight grip. "I wish the judge would delay coming or not come at all."

"Sweetheart," Tate said, "I know you've been worried about having to testify against Bill Sawyer. I want you to know what took place over at the jail this morning."

Elly sat still in the swing. "Please Tate, don't call me Sweetheart. I'm not your sweetheart."

"Listen to me, please," he continued like he hadn't heard her. "I made a deal with Bill Sawyer this morning. I dropped charges against him for attempting to kill me. He sold me his farm and I just watched him leave town for good. He cannot return to this territory."

"Really? There won't be a trial, and I won't have to testify against him in front of the whole town?"

"That's right. The ordeal with him is over."

"Oh Tate," Elly threw her arms around his neck and hugged him tight. She jumped back from him. "Sorry if I hurt your wounds."

"It was worth it, Sweet . . . I'm glad you're relieved that this is over and he's out of our lives for good. He'll make a fresh start, and you don't have to worry about sending him to prison."

"Why did you decide to drop the charges?"

"Sawyer asked me and he said he was sorry. He had been upset and drinking. If he had been sober, he wouldn't have done it. I've known the man a good while and he always minded his own business. I couldn't take a chance that the judge might hang him or send him away for the rest of his life."

"Thank you. I was so worried about that too." She wiped her eyes with the tail of her apron.

"Elly, I have something I would like to ask you. Maybe I should talk with Tim, your only family first, before I speak with you."

"What? You don't have to ask Timmy anything where I'm concerned. I'm my own woman, and I will not have an immature child making any of my life decisions."

"Well, if you're sure. I was hoping you would agree to court me. We need to step out together without arguing or you nursing me. What do you think?"

Elly tried to keep the disappointment off her face. She thought Tate, the man she tried not to love but did more than life itself, was going to ask her to marry him. But instead, he wanted to spend time courting her.

She collected herself and managed a slight turn of the lips. "Well, this is a surprise and kinda sudden. Courting each other could be a good idea. This way we can talk and get to know each other." She glanced out into the yard and peered up at the blue sky. "Yes, I will be honored to court you."

"Good, now, I can call you Sweetheart," he said laughing. "Since I'm in town, may I call on you after lunch to go on a buggy drive? I have something I need to look over."

"Yes, I would enjoy that. Thank you for coming over and giving me the good news about the trial. I'm so happy." She stood to go back inside, but first raised up on our toes and placed a kiss on Tate's cheek.

"Hey, that little peck's not a thank you," he said, then placed his lips over hers and kissed her until her knees went weak. "You're welcome."

Elly floated back into the kitchen with Tate following her.

"I'm going to have a talk with Mattie. I'll see you at lunch. This kitchen always smells so good," Tate said.

"Mattie, are you sure you want to live out on my ranch? There isn't much of a social life out there. No other women yet, so when you aren't working, you'll have to find something to entertain yourself."

"You don't understand. I work here from sunup to sundown every day. Seven days a week for room and board and little pay. Please don't get me wrong. Mrs. Duffy took me and Johnny in and gave me a job and a roof over our heads. But, you see, I don't have much time to spend with Johnny. He is little and needs my attention after school and on the weekends. I feel so bad that I can't go outside with him to play ball or take him hiking. Mrs. Duffy's business is good, but I cook and clean all day. I'm not lazy, but I'm also a country gal. I love riding and taking care of animals. If you hire me, I'll help cook three meals a day and keep your ranch house clean. I can wash and iron, too."

"What about Johnny and his school? He's too young to ride into town by himself?" Tate asked, still unsure about hiring this young lady.

"School doesn't start until nine in the morning. I'm sure your men eat breakfast a lot earlier than that, so after breakfast, I can drive him into town and go after him in the afternoon. I can do this, Mr. Tate."

"Well, it seems you have everything worked out. I personally would enjoy having you and Johnny come and live with us. The ranch life will be good for your brother, and you will have a lot of free time. What will you do with yourself?"

"I love to sew and make lace. My mom and I used to sell some of our lace to the dressmaker in Leesville. I haven't had a minute to myself while working here to do anything for myself."

"When do you think you can start working for me and my pa? You should give Mrs. Duffy time to find another woman to help her."

"I'll work hard to help her find a replacement for me. As soon as she can hire someone, Johnny and I will start working for you."

"I'll pay you thirty-five dollars a month. You and Johnny will both have separate rooms upstairs. We have plenty of ponies on the ranch, so both of you will have a mount that will be yours to ride and care for."

"Oh my, I can't believe this. I have never had so much money that I could call mine. Johnny will have everything he needs and a surprise once in a while. Children need surprises, don't you think?" Mattie could not stop smiling.

"Yes, I do believe that."

After lunch, Tate and Elly took a buggy ride over to Bill Sawyer's farm. Though Elly thought it beautiful, Tate saw a farmhouse in need of repair and fences that needed mending. The windmill had water flowing over the tank onto the ground and the chickens were strutting all over the place. A cow was in pitiful shape. She probably had milk fever, due to not being milked. That crazy Bill should have told the sheriff to have someone check on his animals while in jail.

"Come with me Elly, while I milk the cow. The poor animal has to be hurting something awful." Tate and Elly walked into the barn. Tate placed a leash over the cow's head and told Elly it was for tying the animal to a post. He found a milking stool and straddled it. After washing the cow's teats, he started milking. "It doesn't matter if the milk is clean or not because I'm going to toss it out. But it's just habit to milk a clean animal," he said.

As he started milking the cow, it moaned and stomped her front legs. Elly walked over to the cow's head and spoke quietly in her ear, but the cow became spooked and she kicked her back leg at Tate, hitting him in the stomach. He fell backwards before he could tell Elly to get away from the cow's head. He landed on the flat of his back in a fresh pile of manure.

"What the crap, Elly! Get away from the cow's head."

Elly saw Tate lying in a pile of cow's manure. He looked so funny with the gooey mess framing his shoulders and neck, she couldn't contain her laughter. "Oh, you . . . you look so . . . so nasty." She doubled over with more laughter.

"Why is it every time you're around me, I'm in danger? When I get up from here, your butt is going to be in danger, Missy."

"Me? I didn't kick you or make you fall into that pile." She covered her mouth and stepped backwards.

Tate rolled off the floor and removed his messy shirt. He tossed it on a bale of hay. "You're in for it now, my lady. You'd better run because I am going to blister your behind for spooking that cow."

Elly doubled over with laughter, then turned on her heel and ran. Tate caught up with her, picked her up around the waist and tossed her into a huge pile of hay. She landed with an oomph, and another when he fell down on top of her. "You deserve to be punished, but I have a better way, which will benefit us both." He showered kisses over her neck, chin, eyes and finally her mouth, warm, deep, delicious kisses.

Blood pounded through her veins as a fresh wave of passion traveled through her. She never wanted him to stop. With his good arm, he lifted her hips to press up against his, causing her toes to curl, as she felt his hard body. "Stop, Tate," she tried to say, but his tongue was plunged deep into her mouth. *Oh, Lord, I'm in heaven.*

Finally, Tate freed her swollen lips and said, "Don't regret this,

Elly. In the future, much more will come, but for now, I'll go get cleaned up. I stink."

"Oh, you. You're about as romantic as an old mule."

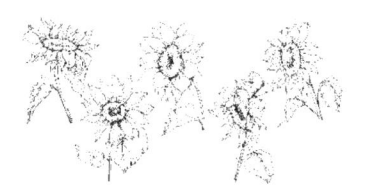

Chapter 32

After a few weeks, Mattie was never happier. She enjoyed working for Tate, Major and Henry. The men were pleased with her work habits. She enjoyed helping Henry cook, and the ranch house was shiny again.

Johnny was happy, too. He followed every step of Tim's, his new best friend. Tim was patient and answered all Johnny's questions. He taught him to saddle, ride, and care for his new pony. Every day, Tim taught Johnny something new on the ranch—how to feed the chickens, slop the hogs and bottle-feed the calves.

After supper when the kitchen was ready for the morning meal, Mattie and Tim sat on the front porch. They shared many wonderful stories of their childhoods but never discussed their bad times.

In the parlor each night, Mattie helped Johnny read over his lessons while she crocheted small white lace. Major joined them and smoked his pipe while reading a book. He had confessed to Tate he enjoyed spending time with this young lady.

Tate began joining the small group in the parlor. Mattie made him think about Elly and how much he enjoyed spending time with her. They were getting along so much better now that they were courting. Mattie and Tim were almost inseparable when they weren't working. Tate had to admit they made a cute couple, and

Tim was good to Johnny. He was pleased that Tim didn't seem to miss drinking and gambling.

"Hey, Tim, this being my first payday, would you like to drive into town with Johnny and me? I want to visit Mrs. Duffy and Elly. I can purchase a few things I need at the dry goods store, too."

As the warm days of summer faded into the cool ones of fall, blooms fell from the lovely wildflowers that bordered the road. Mattie pulled together the edges of the lovely shawl that she had knitted when she was much younger. She wanted to purchase new coats for herself and Johnny, but she couldn't seem to stop smiling.

"What has you so happy this morning, Mattie? You haven't stopped smiling since you climbed into the wagon. Are you that happy to be leaving the ranch?" Tim asked.

"No, silly, I am happy because I can't wait to visit with the girls, and for the first time in my life, I have the means to buy something for myself and Johnny. My folks never had any spare money for necessaries. The church folks were always giving us their hand-me-downs. I never owned a new pair of shoes or a coat. Mama and I made lace to sell so we could buy material to make our personal items. It feels so wonderful to have so much money and to know this time next month, I will have earned more. Johnny will never have to go without like I did as a child. Now, do you understand why I am so happy?"

"Yes, I do. I guess I was lucky and really didn't appreciated it. My pa and mama both worked and gave us nice things to wear, and once in a while, pennies for candy. After Pa left us, my mama kept working along with Elly's help, so we had plenty to eat and clothes to wear." A grimace flashed across his face.

"You didn't mention what you did to help your mama."

"I hate to admit it, but I am realizing what a lazy son I was. I never did anything, but once in a while, I delivered wash to customers. After Mama passed, Elly put me out of our house because I wouldn't help her, like I should have. She tried to make me grow up." Tim looked away.

"It seems like you've changed, to me. You're a good worker on the ranch." Mattie peeked around and made Tim look at her.

"I know, but I have never helped Elly or been there for her. She has always taken care of herself and could never count on me, as the big brother, even though I'm a little younger."

"Well, you know, Tim, it's never too late to let her know you're willing to be here for her. On the wagon train, she shared her feelings with me about you. She was worried that you would be put in jail for gaming with some rough men. So you see, I do know a little about your past."

"I had no idea that Elly even thought about me after I got chased out of Leesville," Tim said, a frown covering his face.

"Believe me. She worried a lot about you, and she's happy now that you're near and working." Mattie reached for his hand.

As they neared the edge of town, Mattie could hardly contain herself. "Now Johnny, I want to visit at the rooming house, and then we'll go shopping. While I am talking with Mrs. Duffy, you may go next door and see your little friend, but don't get dirty."

Tim drove the wagon to the front gate of the rooming house. He leaped to the ground and reached for Mattie, and then helped Johnny down. They walked into the house. "Elly," Tim called, and she came hurrying from the kitchen.

"Mercy, look at the three of you. Tim, you are so tanned and filled out. Henry's cooking must agree with you," laughed Elly.

"Not just Henry's cooking. Mattie here is a great cook, too."

Elly hugged Mattie and wrapped her arms around Johnny. "I believe you have grown a foot, young man," she said.

Johnny hugged her back and said, "I gotta go to the water closet." He raced down the hall while everyone laughed.

Tim took Mattie aside and told her he had some things to do at the livery, and he wanted to say hello to the preacher.

"I will meet you here for lunch, if that is all right with Mrs. Duffy."

"Of course, we will love having you. We'll save three chairs at the table, since we've been having so many customers." Elly smiled and looped her arm into Mattie's and disappeared into the kitchen.

Tim went into the little white church and asked the organist if Preacher Scott was around. "No, Sonny, he is not, but I bet you can find him at the saloon," she said with disgust in her old voice.

Tim left the church and wondered why the preacher would be at the saloon. The old woman made it sound like it might be his second home, even though she didn't actually say that.

Standing on the boardwalk, Tim glanced down the street at the Golden Nugget. He had tried his hand at a card game when he first arrived, but he knew instantly that two of the customers were hustlers. He picked up his few dollars, left the game and he never returned.

He pushed open the bat-winged doors of the saloon and entered the dimly lit room. An older man was playing the piano and two ladies stood at the end of the bar, talking with Sal, the owner. After his eyes adjusted to the dark, he noticed the preacher draped over the bar. Several empty glasses sat in front of him while he sipped another full glass of beer.

"Hello, Scott," Tim eased up next to the man.

The man peeked at Tim through reddened eyes. "Preacher Scott to you," he slurred. "What are you doing in town? Did you come to save your sister's reputation?" Before Tim could answer, he continued, "Boy, did she have me fooled. No wonder she didn't want to have anything to do with a man of God. She ain't nothing but a slut. She could work in here." He said, waving his limp hand at the other bar ladies.

SUNFLOWER BRIDE

Tim jerked the preacher up off the bar. He stood him straight and hit him as hard as he could with his right fist. The preacher landed on his back. He shook his head and laughed like a fool.

"Why did you do that? You can't take the truth about your sister? Ask any of these men in here. Several of them found her and that Maynard fellow wrapped in each other's arms in a cave after that man who kidnapped her had his way with her. She was already broken in for him."

Tim jumped down and straddled his chest with his fist drawn back, prepared to hit the foul-talking man in the mouth.

"Go ahead. Ask any man in here. They'll tell you the truth."

Tim stood up slowly with both of his fists clenched. His right fist felt like it was broken. He turned to big Sal. "What he's saying, is any of it the truth?"

"Now, Tim. The posse was looking for your sister after Bill Sawyer kidnapped her. Tate was hurt bad. The men did find them in a cave wrapped in each other's arms, but like I said, Tate was hurt bad."

"Not near as bad as he's going to be," Tim said under his breath but loud enough for Sal to hear.

As Tim gathered himself together, he asked Sal. "What in the hell happened to our good preacher? He's the sorriest *padre* I've ever seen. I hope he won't be in the pulpit tomorrow."

Tim rushed out of the saloon and headed straight to the rooming house. Once he entered, he went to the kitchen and grabbed Elly's free hand and dragged her out the back door. He didn't stop until they were away from the house.

"What are you doing?" Elly screamed at her brother. "Turn me loose this minute." She struggled to free herself from his strong grip.

"I want the truth out of you and nothing less, you got it? Were you with Tate in a cave cuddled together for all the men in town to see?" Elly's mouth fell open. "Tell me the truth, or so help me, I'll go and beat it out of your lover."

"Tim, where did you hear that gossip?"

"Is it the truth?" he demanded without keeping his voice down.

"Well, we were together in the cave when the men found us, but Tate was hurt bad. I had hurt him when I pulled him off his horse."

"I know you and Tate are courting, but when does he plan to make an honest woman out of you. Your reputation is in shreds. All the men are laughing about your situation. That preacher man is drunk at the saloon and he's spewing lies all about you and that Sawyer fellow who kidnapped you. He's saying that he had his way with you and you allowed it."

"What? That's not true. Tim, you can't believe that. Tate dropped the charges against him and he's gone. Tate would have killed him if that man had harmed me."

"Speaking of Tate, sister of mine, you both will be getting married tomorrow if I have my way. Prepare yourself. I'm going to see him now." Tim stormed into the house and asked Mrs. Duffy if she would tell Mattie to drive herself and Johnny back to the ranch. He would rent a horse at the livery.

Elly came into the house as white as a sheet. "What's wrong child?" Mrs. Duffy asked.

"Tim. He's acting like a wild man. He's going to see Tate and make him marry me . . . tomorrow. I've never seen him act like this before."

"He's acting like a big brother who just heard rumors about his sister and his boss. You should be proud of him, Elly. I am. He has finally grown up."

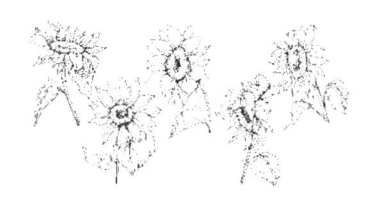

Chapter 33

Tate was standing at the corral watching Slim train a new pony. "I want to have this young colt trained before Christmas. It's a present for Johnny," Tate said.

"That young man has managed to get into all of our hearts," Slim said. "I think Tim is over the moon with Mattie. And she's fond of him."

"You're right. You know, Slim, I was thinking about offering Tim Bill Sawyer's farm to oversee for us. If he proves himself, I might even lease it to him while he's working the land. Be a nice home for a young family. What do you think?"

"Elly would be happy if she knew he was settled somewhere close," Slim replied.

"Speaking of the devil, here comes Tim now. I thought he left with Mattie and Johnny in the buggy this morning."

Tim was riding faster than he should have been when he reached Tate and Slim at the corral fence. He leaped from the horse and landed in front of the two of them. Before Tate saw it coming, Tim swung his right fist as hard as he could catching Tate under the chin. Tate rocked backwards into the fence, which kept him from falling to the ground. He righted himself.

"Oh, my hand," Tim yelled. "I think I've broken it."

"What the hell?" Tate said rubbing his chin, then seized Tim's collar and gave him a good shake. "What's the matter with you? Have you lost your senses?"

Tim stood holding his fist between his legs moaning.

Reaching for Tim's hand, Tate examined it. "You didn't do that hitting me. Who else did you hit?"

"Turn me loose before I get a gun and shoot you. I know about you and Elly being found in the cave together. You've ruined her reputation and now you're going to pay. You will marry her tomorrow!" Tim held his fist, looking like he wanted to cry.

"Lord help me," mumbled Tate and rubbed his chin. "Slim, bring this big brother into the house while I get Major. He's good at setting bones. I believe this young hero has broken his hand."

"Pa," Tate yelled into the barn. "Come and help Tim. He may have broken his right hand."

Major glanced up from pitching hay. "Did you say Tim broke his hand?" He shielded his eyes from the sun and saw his son's face. "What in heaven's name happened to your face? We need to put a cold compact on that before it swells more."

"Pa," Tate said, "Tim went to town and heard the ugly rumors about me and Elly. He's upset and demanding that I marry Elly tomorrow."

"Can't say I blame the boy one bit. I would be upset too, if she was my sister. I don't think the marriage can take place tomorrow, but I feel like Tim. You should have married her weeks ago. Come on, I'll look at the young man's hand."

"I can tell you now that Elly and I are not going to be railroaded into marriage because Tim or the townspeople demand it. I love her and I'll decide the date and time," Tate shouted.

Two weeks later, Elly stood at the back of the church, shifting from one foot to the other. Her nerves threatened to jump out of her body. The sight of Major helped her to gain control of herself and feel a little less stressed. Mattie stood in front of Elly twisting and swishing her long skirt, sharing stolen glances with Tim.

Major took her palms in his, leaned down and placed a kiss on her rosy cheek. "You, my dear, are a beautiful bride any man would be proud to marry," he said. "Becky would have been so pleased to know you were wearing her gown." His display of concern for her was what every girl dreamed their father would have for them on her wedding day. Major cleared his throat, bringing Elly's focus back to the present. "Are you ready to marry my son?"

"The question should be is he ready to marry me? You and I both know he's being forced to save my reputation." Tears threatened to spill from behind her eyelids. She looked toward the front of the church where Tate stood beside the preacher from Waterville. Preacher Cunningham had been dismissed and the sheriff had telegraph Reverend Wallace in the next town to come and perform the ceremony.

"Miss Elly, I know my boy. Nothing would make him do something he didn't want to do. He could have found a different solution to this problem if he really wanted to do so. My son loves you." Major tilted her chin to face him. "I've got to go stand next to Tate."

Major bit the inside of his mouth to keep a somber expression as he watched Tate's bride. His sweet wife would have approved of Tate's choice. His Rebecca, whom he called Becky, was here today in his thoughts, in his heart, and with Elly in her lovely gown. Earlier he'd stood to the side of the church entrance and watched Elly shift from one foot to the other as the ladies straightened her dress, his wife's and Tate's mama's bridal gown. His precious Rebecca's grandmother and mama from the old country had sat many days and nights sewing the tiny jewels on the front of the lovely gown's bodice. Some of the jewels came from her grandmother's jewelry and her mama's wedding necklace. The dress had to be altered a little, but it looked beautiful on Elly.

Tate stood ramrod straight at the front of the church. He could see Elly fidgeting in the back and talking with his pa. Elly—a woman he never planned to love but did with everything in him. Being fearful of marriage and never wanting to be hogtied to a woman, this day was never in his plans for the future. Especially to a clumsy woman, ignorant of the outdoors, and a smart mouth to boot. The two months on the wagon train and the weeks of being her patient had changed his mind, which defied all logic. He smiled and studied her face from the front of the church. What was life going to be like from this day forward?

The sound from the old organ shook Tate back to the present. He and his pa watched Mattie stroll toward the front of the church. She smiled at all the men who packed the pews. Tate's pa whispered from the side of his mouth, "I bet there'll be another wedding soon if that gal has her way."

Elly took her brother's arm while the banker's wife began *The Wedding March*. The old organist offered the couple a toothless grin as the couple came slowly down the aisle. Everyone jumped up from their pew to witness the most beautiful bride this old town had ever seen walk toward her groom.

"I wouldn't mind being held at gunpoint and made to marry that little gal," one of the old cowboys said in a loud gest. Another man jabbed him in the ribs with his bony elbow. "Quiet, you old fool."

Elly sucked in her breath and fought back the instant tears that threatened to spill over her cheeks. His remark was a reminder that Tate was being forced to marry her in order to save her reputation. The men promised to keep silent about finding them wrapped in each other's arms in the cave. So much for keeping quiet, Elly thought.

Elly strolled beside Tim who had grown into a handsome man. His new dark suit was catching the eye of Mattie, who had fallen in love with him. He held Elly's arm in the tight crook of his arm, not giving her a chance to retreat.

Elly sniffed back her tears and smoothed her lovely dress with sparkling jewels on the bodice and soft lace around the neck. She glanced down at the pair of soft pink slippers Tate had delivered to her as a special wedding gift. Where in the world had he gotten them on such short notice? She'd ask him later, but for now, she was thrilled to have the thoughtful gift.

When the music stopped, Elly stood next to Tate, and Tim had taken his seat on the front pew next to Mrs. Duffy. Was this a dream or a nightmare?

Everything had happen so fast. Tate had come to the rooming house and told her that they would be married in two weeks. No proposal, no getting down on his knees in front of her declaring his love. Nothing but a demand.

"What?" she had screamed.

"If you don't like it, too bad. This is your brother's command and we don't have a say-so about it." Then he was gone, and all the fuss and planning began.

Mrs. Duffy looked tired but pleased with how beautiful Elly looked. She and Mrs. Langley had worked night and day altering the wedding dress and preparing enough food for the reception, which would be held in the parlor of the rooming house.

The major beamed at Tate. He'd told Elly he knew in his heart she was the perfect mate for his son. He said a rancher needed a hard-working wife, and Elly would do just fine, even though she was a city girl.

Preacher Wallace cleared his throat to get Elly's focus back to him. The older man spoke directly to Tate and Elly. You could hear a penny drop in the church. He spoke first to Tate about the responsibility of being a good provider, then to Elly about being a good helpmate and an obedient wife. She swallowed hard, praying that God wouldn't strike her down on this very spot for lying. She wasn't sure about the obey part, but she nodded anyway.

The minister continued until both had spoken their vows, loud and clear. Elly had never planned to marry, but if she did, it would be for love, not for security and respectability. Deep down in her heart, she did love this bullheaded man who stood beside her. Having to marry today could have been worse. She might have had to marry that mean Bill Sawyer or that Pastor Scott. Thank the good Lord she was spared that disgrace.

"You may kiss your bride," announced Reverend Wallace.

Tate turned Elly toward him, leaned in and whispered, "This is the first of many to come, my dear," he dipped her back and planted a passionate kiss on her lips.

Snickering, giggling, and hoarse laughter broke out from the pews. Tate wrapped his good arm around Elly's waist and pulled her into a close embrace. He grinned just like he had won first place in a horse race. They were torn away from each other by all the well-wishers and hugs from the single men in the audience. Elly wished to be back with Tate as she was passed from one man to another.

"That's enough, fellows," Tate finally said. "Head over to Mrs. Duffy's for some food and cold beer." Once Elly was turned loose from the last man, Tate reached for her hand. "Are you all right?"

"Yes, I'm fine. I wasn't prepared for all the men. How are you doing? I noticed some of the ladies from the saloon and a few widows held your attention." She laughed and headed up the aisle.

"Wait a minute. We have to sign the marriage license in the church office. Come on, then we'll go to meet our guests at the reception."

Tate signed the marriage license, *Tate Conrad Maynard* and Elly's signature read, *Eleanor Susan Eddy*. He read her full name. "Susan? I like it."

Elly grinned up at him and said, "Conrad. A bold name. You look like a Conrad." Both of them shared a laugh. This was the first intimate moment of their lives together. They had learned something new about each other. She reached up and placed a kiss on Tate's cheek and whispered, "I love you."

Tate stared into Elly's eyes, not believing what she had said. This was the first time she had said those words to him. Just as he reached for her to reply, Tim and Mattie hurried up to them.

"Oh Elly, Tate, we are both so happy for you and for ourselves, too." Mattie giggled and Tim beamed. "Sis, Mattie has agreed to marry me. Can you believe it?"

Elly hugged Mattie tight. "I couldn't be more pleased. Why didn't you tell me sooner?"

"We didn't want to take anything away from your wedding day by casting light on us. This is your special day, and we will have ours soon."

"Congratulations, Tim, Mattie. We need to get to our reception. Come with us," said Tate as he looped his arm around his new wife's waist.

In one corner of the reception hall, men gathered to tell wedding-night jokes, and one man was making crude remarks about Elly. A short mousey fellow named Wilbur, who had way too much to drink, was talking about Elly being alone with her kidnapper. "All the women say the bride is as pure as the Virgin Mary, but the groom will soon learn if that's the gospel truth."

The men's laughter dried up when Tate slipped into their circle. He lifted Wilbur off his feet by the scruff of his neck and suspended him in the air. After a rough shake, he lowered him to the floor.

"Little man, if this wasn't my wedding day, I would stuff your behind down the town well and leave you there. Do you get my drift," he said, while turning him to face the others. "This had better be the last I ever hear anything bad about my lovely Sunflower bride. Nothing, and I mean nothing, happened between Elly and me in the cave. I was unconscious, for gosh sakes, and nothing took place between Elly and Sawyer while she was alone with him. I hope I never have to mention this again." Tate glared at the men, then he shook Wilber one more time and patted him on the shoulder. "Have I made myself clear?"

Many 'yes sirs' and heads bobbed up and down as the men went their separate ways. Tate walked away in search of his lovely bride. He found her over by the punch bowl, and he pulled her into his arms for what he hoped would be their final dance.

"What was going on over in that corner of the parlor?" Elly asked.

"Just a private joke about a handsome groom and his beautiful bride. Are you ready to go home, Mrs. Maynard

Chapter 34

Once they arrived at the ranch, Tate carried Elly across the threshold into the empty house. Major had planned to stay at the rooming house, and Henry and the other men wouldn't be home until sunrise.

Elly stood in her new bedroom while Tate made sure that the doors were locked and the fires were banked.

When he entered the bedroom, he grinned. "Do you like it?"

"Oh Tate, this is a lovely room, but wasn't this your old room?"

"Yes, Mattie helped me redecorate it for you and me."

"I will have to tell her how much I like it." Elly said as she approached the window and examined the curtains.

Tate removed his dress coat while watching Elly in the mirror. She had not moved. He wondered if she was even breathing.

"Sweetheart," he said softly. "I have a confession to make to you."

Elly spun around, her brow furrowed.

"The last two weeks I have deliberately stayed away from you. I know you were scared and angry. My proposal wasn't anything a girl could write home about, but I, too, was afraid."

"You . . . afraid?"

"Yes, me, afraid. Afraid you would say no and pack up your

belongings and leave town."

He approached her and took her hands. "This is my confession. I was never forced into this marriage. Tim would like to think that he made me marry you, to right a wrong done to his sister. But I married you because I have loved you ever since I rescued you from that nasty ditch. No man, not even Tim, could ever make me do something I didn't want to do. I had never thought about marrying one of our wagon-train brides. You had said over and over that you weren't going to be a Sunflower bride." Tate squeezed her fingertips. "I wasn't sure if I would survive the trip to make you change your mind."

"Oh Tate. I wasn't that bad, was I?" Elly smiled and leaned into his hard body. "I loved you, even when you acted like an overbearing brute. I tried not to, but you were so impossible not to love." She stood on her tiptoes and whispered in his ear, "I love you so much."

"Now that we understand each other, let's go to bed," Tate said raising his eyebrows. "I know you've been through a lot today. Are you hungry?" Tate asked.

"No, how about you?"

"Hungry only for you." He ran his hand through her raven hair, then removed the bridal flowers. Taking her hand, he kissed each finger, causing chills to run down her back. She knew he was taking his time trying to calm her nerves. The good Lord knew she was scared to death of the marriage act between a man and woman.

He twisted her slowly around and unfastened the tiny pearl buttons at her neck. Leaning down, he kissed the back of her smooth neck and her ears. She stood as still as a statue. She felt his hands in her hair as he removed the pins, allowing them to fall to the floor. She leaned back into him, but he moved her to face him. He lowered his lips to hers and kissed her deeply. She whimpered as he worked his charm over her body. He left her standing near the bed.

Tate removed the few flowers that had been spread over their pillows and turned back the lovely quilt. He unbuttoned his white shirt and slipped it over a chair. Then he slowly removed his shiny boots and his new socks.

She stepped out of her wedding dress, steeling herself for what was to come when he removed his pants. *Lord help me,* she thought. He was naked from the waist down and the sight of his body startled her. She had no idea what to do next.

"Where are your long johns?" she said in a squeaky voice.

"I never wear anything to bed. I have always slept naked. Do you mind?"

Elly shook her head as she turned away from him to remove her chemise and corset. She didn't attempt to remove her bloomers as she reached for her new muslin gown that Mattie had made her for a wedding gift. Tate reached out and took it from her. "You won't need this tonight or those." He nodded toward her bloomers.

Elly didn't comment. She was trying to keep her eyes from his naked torso. He was tan, almost bronze, from his waist up and snow white below. The contrast astonished her. His body was smooth and muscular, not even a blemish except for the purplish scars on his shoulder and back, which were fading nicely.

Tate took her hand and led her to the four-poster bed. "Tonight, I don't want anything between us—no anger, no secrets, no clothes."

She moaned, "Oh God, help me. I'm afraid of the pain that I've been warned about. Are you going to hurt me?" she asked and appeared more like a scared child than a woman.

"I'm the only man in this bed tonight. You don't have to fear me. It's all right, sweetheart. It'll be over soon. I'll try to be gentle. You have to help me by relaxing your lovely body."

Suddenly it was all over and he was a liar. He had invaded her body with his, and the pain was nearly unbearable. She'd gasp and opened her eyes to see him smiling down at her. He wasn't getting up or moving to her side. "Enjoy it, honey, there's more to come."

"Please, no more pain." She mumbled, but soon came a

wonderful feeling deep in her body. She began to feel something different. In a few seconds, she felt pure pleasure as he moved slowly. When she thought she would die from the joy she was feeling, he collapsed onto her, nearly smothering her with his body.

"I'm sorry, honey. I meant to go slow, but I have waited so long to be with you—I love you."

She lay still and then rubbed his muscular back and shoulders. He had finally said the words again she longed to hear. He loved her. His face was pressed between her neck and face, and he was breathing hard. Once, he raised his face and looked into her eyes. Instead of pushing his large frame off her small body, she couldn't resist the urge to hold him. She was complete, Tate's wife, the last Sunflower Bride and she hadn't killed him --yet.

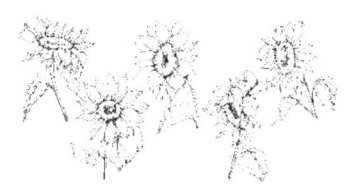

Epilogue

Elly sent up a silent prayer that this would be the last time she heaved in the chamber pot. She flopped down on the cold floor and wiped her mouth. This was the third morning in a row that she smelled Henry's wonderful breakfast, then raced to the bedroom's water closet to throw up her guts.

After the second morning, she realized that she hadn't had a monthly flow since they married nearly three months ago. She was going to have a baby. The thrill took second place because she was sure she was going to throw up the baby.

Nearly three months of blissful marriage to Tate had been wonderful, but they hadn't discussed having children. With all the action in their bedroom, something surely had to result in this wonderful event. Had Tate noticed anything different about her body? Realizing she was going to have a child made her more aware of her swelling breasts and her thickening waistline.

Men never noticed anything until you refused them something that they wanted. Just like children, Elly thought. With Christmas only a week away, she would wait and give this wonderful news to Tate as a Christmas present. She knew in her heart that he'd be excited about the coming baby. Maybe a little Tate in the near future whom they could call, "Conrad."

As she sat on the cold floor in the water closet, her thoughts went to Tim and Mattie. They might be having a baby soon, too. She thought of the young couple sneaking away from the ranch one night and traveling to the next town. They woke up Reverend Wallace and insisted that he perform a ceremony. Tate wanted to know why they had eloped. Mattie responded they needed their money for the future. She was certainly thrifty with money, something Tim had never learned until now.

Elly stood and placed the lid on the chamber pot. She needed to dress, eat a piece of toast and have a cup of coffee. As she dressed, she thought about the night that Tate presented the Sawyer's farm to the young couple. She remembered his words. "You may lease the farm for a year, and if it is profitable, you may buy it, if that is your soul desire. You will be living next door to us, which I know will make my beautiful wife happy." Tate was always doing things to please her, and he was a good man to his close friends and neighbors.

After Elly dressed, nibbled on the toast and drank her coffee, she was ready for the day. The morning sickness had disappeared, like it had never happened. Hearing laughter coming from outside near the corral area, she hurried to see what the excitement was all about.

Johnny had discovered his new pony that was to be his Christmas present from Major and Tate. The men had tried to keep the colt in the back pasture, but the little fellow had followed some of the herd up to the main corral fence.

"Look, Aunt Elly, look. This pony is all mine," Johnny called to her. Ever since Mattie's and Tim's marriage, they told him to call Tate and Elly *uncle* and *aunt*, which pleased them both.

"This was supposed to be my Christmas present, but my pony wanted me to have him early. Ain't that something?"

"He seems like a smart pony. Have you selected a name for him yet?" Elly asked and rubbed the animal's neck.

"Not yet, but I'm going to think on it. He has to have a name like I have to have a saddle. I don't have my very own yet," he said, his eyes brightening. The smart little fellow had figured the saddle and other things related to the pony would be under the Christmas tree.

"Good morning, Sweetheart," called Tate. "We're all going to ride over to Tim's and let Johnny show off his new pony to his sister. Go in the house and get a jacket so you won't be too cold. Hurry now and I'll help you up in the saddle of this gentle mare. I picked her out just for you."

"No, thank you. You fellows just go without me." Seeing the disappointment in Tate's expression, she said, "Now Tate, I told you before that my horseback riding days are over." She spun to walk back to the house, but Tate snatched her hand and brought her around to face him.

"Listen to me, Elly dearest." Tate clenched his teeth and held a smile for all the men to see. "You are a country gal now, and country girls know how to ride. Therefore, you will continue your lessons today, like I promised on the wagon train."

"And on the wagon train, I told you that I would not get back on a horse by myself. I can go anywhere I need to in a buggy or in our new carriage." She attempted again to walk away, but he held her hand tighter.

Shaking his hand, she tried to get away. "Turn me loose, you big overbearing—" Tate slapped his hand over her mouth and stepped closer to her.

"Now, Sweetheart, don't make me embarrass you out here in front of Johnny and the men," Tate said, still maintaining a smile.

Johnny was over by the horse trough, letting his pony splash water over his boots and the surrounding ground. He frowned at the heated words between Tate and Aunt Elly, just like the arguments between his sister and Tim.

Elly pointed her finger at Tate's chest. She jabbed him over and over as he moved away, one giant step backwards at a time toward Johnny. Tate was grinning at her as she spewed unladylike words at him for trying to tell her what she would or wouldn't do. He seemed to enjoy getting her all riled up.

Johnny had to jump out of the way when one of Tate's boots slipped in the muddy water in front of the horse trough and he lost his balance. Elly jabbed him once more, and he fell backwards into the ice cold water. His tall frame went under, and he came up sputtering. Elly stepped closer to her splashing husband, trying to hide her wide smile. "You look so funny," she said.

The men jumped off their mounts and raced over to help Tate, careful not to allow the icy water to get on them. Elly turned and ran back to the house laughing.

"Elly!" Tate screamed and slapped the water with his large hands. He wiped water from his face and yelled for all the world to hear. "Thank God the water isn't deep enough for me to drown."

The men pulled Tate to a standing position as cold water dripped from his tall frame, "One day," he said, "that little woman of mine is going to be the death of me."

Biography of Linda Sealy Knowles

Linda Sealy Knowles enjoys writing western romance stories. Writing is a God-gifted talent she never knew she had until she turned sixty-eight. At the golden age of seventy-four, with her ninth book in print, she couldn't be happier. Linda resides in Niceville, Florida, near her two grown children and three wonderful teenage granddaughters. Linda hails from the Satsuma/Saraland area of Mobile, Alabama.

Social Media contacts

Amazon Author Page

https://www.amazon.com/author/lindasealyknowles

Email

Lindajk@cox.net

Goodread.com/

Instagram

Facebook

Facebook Blog

https://writerlindasealyknowles.com/2019/04/24/what/an/exciting/day/

Other books by Linda Sealy Knowles

The Maxwell Saga in Limason, Texas

Journey to Heaven Knows Where, Book1

Hannah's Way, Book 2

The Secret, Book 3

Bud's Journey Home, Book 4

Always Jess, Book 5

Kathleen of Sweetwater, Texas

Abby's New Life

Joy's Cowboy

The Importance of Reviews

Reviews are like the foundation of a good book. Please share your experience while reading my story and meeting my characters. Good or bad, it is your opinion, and I learn from your comments. Publishers love to read your thoughts and opinions, too. Take an extra few minutes and express your thoughts and feelings about the book you just read on Amazon.com.

Made in the USA
Columbia, SC
01 November 2021